LOST TO THE NIGHT

THE BROTHERHOOD SERIES - BOOK 1

ADELE CLEE

She walks in beauty, like the night
Of cloudless climes and starry skies,
And all that's best of dark and bright
Meets in her aspect and her eyes;
Thus mellow'd to that tender light
Which Heaven to gaudy day denies

George Gordon, Lord Byron
(1788–1824)

CHAPTER 1

A TAVERN IN SCHILTACH, BAVARIA,
1818

*A*lexander Cole's blood gushed through his veins like hot, molten lava. The sweet fire that consumed him had nothing to do with the buxom wench at his side, merrily massaging his manhood.

"You like it?" She giggled playfully, shaking her fleshy wares as if they were easy to miss.

Alexander groaned as she tightened her grip and nuzzled his ear. Yet he continued to stare at the woman sitting on the opposite side of the tavern.

He had noticed her walk in minutes earlier. She'd not ordered a drink but sat shrouded in a sapphire-blue cloak boldly watching him. Was she aware of the eager hand pleasuring him beneath the table? Was that the reason she stared?

Alexander.

Despite downing copious amounts of wine and ale, his mind suddenly stilled, the noise of the boisterous crowd drowned out by a soft sibilant whisper. He heard his name echoing through the silent chambers of his mind: a siren's call —luring him, drawing him, forcing him to follow.

Alexander.

In a bid to locate Reeves and Lattimer he glanced around the crude room, its stone walls and low beams relics of a bygone era. Reeves was asleep on the wooden bench, his fingers wrapped around the handle of a tankard as he cuddled it to his chest. Two weeks of drunken debauchery had definitely taken its toll. Through the cloudy mist of stale tobacco smoke, he spotted Lattimer climbing the stairs. The eager wench was pulling him up by his hand, his reluctance due to an unsteady gait as opposed to a lack of enthusiasm.

Alexander.

He heard his name again, the seductive tones of a woman's sated whisper dragging him back to the mysterious creature across the room.

The wench at his side continued pumping, yet his focus moved to the enchantress who had lowered the hood of her cloak to reveal a mane of silky golden tresses. He sucked in a breath, captivated by her full red lips and porcelain skin. Drinking in the sight, he groaned as she put the tip of her tongue to her lips and moistened the entrance to her mouth.

Compelled by a sudden wave of disgust, he slapped his hand over the wench's sweaty fingers.

"Oh, you want to help."

"No," he growled, pushing her hand away, his desire for a stranger the motivating factor.

He threw a few coins onto the table and hastily buttoned the fall of his breeches.

The golden-haired goddess smiled, raised her hood and moved gracefully to the door before escaping out into the night.

As though connected by an invisible thread, he followed her to the door and yanked it open, ignoring the wench's cries of protest—jealousy being a trait he despised.

Rain lashed against the solid oak door. He winced as it pelted his face, quick and sharp, almost knocking him back.

He could just make out his quarry crossing the muddy road, heading towards a carriage. Pulling his coat more firmly across his chest, he snuggled into it and braved the weather—some strange force urging him to take the next step.

The lady glanced over her shoulder and beckoned him to follow. Whether it was intrigue, lust or a powerful primal hunger that drew him to her carriage, he did not know. She climbed into the conveyance and closed the door, yet the driver made no move to depart and sat staring off into the distance waiting for a command.

Alexander stumbled up to the window and peered inside to find his beauty sitting back in the seat, her cape open, exposing the upper curve of her breasts. Shaping his mouth in an attempt to form a word, he seemed to have lost the ability of speech.

The temptress smiled and opened the door. "Are you coming in?"

He climbed inside, the carriage lurching forward before he'd had a chance to take his seat.

They raced through the cobbled streets at breakneck speed, up along the path curving through the forest. He thought to seduce his vixen with salacious banter, but his tongue felt thick, his lips swollen and numb.

She watched him, her hands resting in her lap, never moving, yet his body reacted to the touch of her wandering gaze. It felt as though her fingers clawed away at him, scrabbling over his chest, tugging at his clothes, freeing him from the confines of his breeches. As the imaginary assault tormented him, he could smell the heady scent of his arousal, and he struggled to draw breath.

"You respond to me well, Alexi," she whispered. "But now you must sleep."

Sleep was the last thing on his mind, but his lids grew heavy, his surroundings hazy, black.

Alexander had experienced many vivid dreams in his life. The best ones always involved forbidden carnal pleasures: taking the vicar's wife, his daughter, both together.

But this dream was like no other.

He recalled climbing a narrow stone staircase curling up to a tower. The sound of teasing feminine laughter pulled him up. As did the potent smell of exotic incense drifting out from the doorway. The seductive mist creeping towards him felt like invisible fingers massaging his shoulders, determined to relax him, to seduce him.

Time skipped forward.

He lay stretched out on the canopy bed: a monstrous structure of wooden pillars and grotesque carvings. Two naked women fumbled with his breeches, stripping him bare, their eager hands and mouths bringing him close to climax. But when his enchantress entered the room they scurried away, the sound of their whimpering dampening his desire.

"I read your thoughts, Alexi," she said, her cape billowing behind her as she walked towards the bed. "You like power. You like to control. You have had many women, no?"

Alexander nodded.

"After tonight, you will no longer be able to hide behind your chivalrous mask, behind your polished words and fancy clothes." She crawled onto the bed to straddle him while he watched helplessly. "Your depravity will be your constant companion now."

As she bent down to kiss him, he felt a coldness sweep through him followed by a raging fire as her tongue and teeth licked and nipped his neck. Something sharp punctured his skin—then he felt lost, alone.

Then he felt nothing.

CHAPTER 2

*E*velyn Bromwell pulled the thick tartan blanket over her legs and shivered. "I've never known it be so cold." She thrust her gloved hands under the thick material as the wind rocked the carriage. "Not in April."

"Well, you know what they say about the weather," Aunt Beatrice replied, her hands nestled inside a mink muff. "In like a lion, out like a lamb."

Evelyn frowned. "How can it be in like a lion when the month is almost over? Besides, I thought the saying referred to March."

"It applies the other way around, too, and the Welsh often use it for April. If you recall, it was rather mild early on."

The wind rattled the window just to prove a point, the drawn-out howl like an ominous warning.

"More like in with a whistle, out with a whirlwind." Evelyn chuckled.

A dull thud on the carriage roof caused them both to gasp. They froze in anticipation, as though a lion really was about to burst in through the door.

"Either the coachman has fallen off his perch, or the

forest is tumbling down around us," Evelyn whispered, not wishing to tempt fate. "I'd pop my head out and take a look, but knowing my luck, I'd be slapped in the face by a stray branch. Somehow, I don't expect Mr. Sutherby will want to propose to a lady when she's sporting a blackened eye."

Aunt Beatrice smiled. "I think you could sprout a potato from your nose and still Mr. Sutherby would be smitten."

Mr. Sutherby might be smitten, but Evelyn wasn't.

Oh, she was hardly in a position to complain. A handsome gentleman with an affable character and a sizeable fortune wanted to marry her. It sounded perfect. For a gentleman to embody all three traits was a rare find indeed. It's what her parents dreamed of. It's what they would have wanted.

The only thing that could make Mr. Sutherby more desirable was a title. But such far-fetched aspirations were only to be found in fairy tales, not dreams.

The wind gave a mournful cry, and the carriage rocked from side to side.

"Do you think we'll make it to the inn?" Evelyn asked, feeling a little wary. "I think the forest is the worst place to be in a storm."

"It's worse out at sea, waves as tall as houses they say. But we've only a few miles to the inn. We'll bed down for the night, have a late start and be at Mytton Grange by luncheon." Aunt Beatrice removed her hand from her muff and patted Evelyn's knee. "Let's not think about it anymore. Soon we will be tucked up nice and snug in our beds. Perhaps if we talk, we'll distract our minds."

Evelyn groaned inwardly. She didn't want to talk about Mr. Sutherby, but it was the only subject to interest her aunt.

"Of course, once Mr. Sutherby—"

"Can we talk about something else?"

Her aunt narrowed her gaze but then gave a knowing smile. "I understand. You're nervous. It's to be expected.

Very well, I shall think of a different topic to occupy our thoughts."

Her aunt fell silent while she stared at a point beyond Evelyn's shoulder.

Feeling somewhat impatient and having never ventured as far as the New Forest before, Evelyn asked, "Do you know anything about the area? Any exciting tales from ancient folklore?"

"Not really." Her aunt sighed. "Though there are tales of the Earl of Hale. He lives a mile or two from here. No doubt you've heard of him."

Evelyn pondered the question. "The Earl of Hale. The name sounds familiar. Do you mean the gentleman who's said to be horribly disfigured?"

"Well, that's what folk say."

"But you've never seen him?"

"No, no." Her aunt shook her head vigorously as though the thought was abhorrent. "No one has."

"Then how do they know he's disfigured?"

Her aunt shrugged. "I'm sure someone must have seen him at some point. They say he had an accident abroad. When the old earl died, they say he wouldn't set foot near the grave. He hung back in the shadows, his collar raised up to his cheekbones, the brim of his hat touching the tip of his nose."

"To hide his terrible scars, I imagine."

"Some say he'd been standing there all night."

Evelyn was so intrigued she'd almost forgotten they were in danger of being blown away. She imagined all sorts of hideous marks: raised pink rivulets running down his cheek, an earlobe missing, an eye drooping and sagging. Had the earl been injured in a fight, or perhaps a fire?

"And he lives not far from here?" she said, trying to banish her macabre thoughts.

"Yes. In an old Elizabethan house in a clearing."

They fell silent for a moment.

Aunt Beatrice's head shot up, and she gave a little gasp. "Have I told you about the *Pixey* mounds? Well, that's what the locals call them. You'll find them dotted all around the forest."

"Someone must have seen him recently."

Aunt Beatrice jerked her head back. "Who, the *Pixey*? The mounds are old burial sites. I don't think they've got anything to do with real pixies."

"Not the pixies—the earl. Someone must have seen him since the accident."

Her aunt shrugged. "Well, I guess we'll never—"

A sudden tremor shook the carriage. It swayed left and right, throwing them out of their seats. The horses' high-pitched neighs were long and loud, interspersed with the coachman's cries and curses. They scrambled to hold on to the leather straps as a sharp crack was followed by a violent bump. The carriage tipped, throwing them to the left as they hit a ditch.

They continued to fall, crashing down onto the forest floor, the sound of splintering wood lost amongst their shrieks and screams. Evelyn's head rebounded off the inside wall, once, twice, the third time making it hard to focus. Everything before her grew hazy—everything went black.

Evelyn opened her eyes and blinked rapidly. She had no notion how long she'd lain there in a crumpled heap curled next to the body of her aunt. She felt no immediate pain, other than a pounding behind her eyes.

"Aunt Beatrice," she whispered to the woman lying next to her. "Aunt Beatrice."

She waited for a sign of life: a cough, a gasp, a sigh. But the world was deathly silent. Flexing her fingers and lifting her arms to check her limbs were able, Evelyn grabbed the edge of the seat and tried to stand. The carriage had tipped onto its side, the window above them framing a mass of purple and black storm clouds.

Dragging herself up on her feet, she turned to examine her aunt's body. Lying on her side with her head facing away, her aunt was too quiet, too still. She patted the woman's legs beneath her skirt, moved up to check her arm and shoulder. Nothing appeared to be broken. Then she noticed her aunt's head pressed against the shattered window. When Evelyn pushed her hand under her aunt's cheek, it felt slimy and sticky.

With a gasp she pulled her hand away, her pale pink glove now stained a deep shade of red.

There was blood, too much blood.

She needed to get help quick.

Pushing the carriage door open, she climbed out and lowered herself down to the ground.

An uprooted tree trunk blocked the road, the knobbly branches disappearing into the forest. No doubt this was what had startled the horses. Miraculously, the team of four were unharmed. They stood quietly waiting for instruction, oblivious to the disaster that had just unfolded or the upturned wreckage behind them.

Evelyn scanned the area looking for the driver and spotted the burly figure lying sprawled out on the ground. She raced over, touched the back of his coat and rocked him gently hoping to rouse a response.

Nothing.

Her aunt's words drifted into her thoughts.

It's just a few miles to the inn.

After giving each horse a reassuring pat and a few calming words, she wrapped her cloak around her, climbed over the trunk and hurried down the road.

She tried to run, desperate to reach the inn before dusk. It would be difficult to find help come nightfall. And the biting wind only made her task more arduous.

When she came to a fork in the road, she stopped. Taking a moment to catch her breath, she examined her options. Surely the road ahead led to the inn. It appeared to be wider, the well-worn grooves suggesting regular use.

So why was she drawn to the narrow, overgrown lane?

Why did she feel a strange tug in her stomach at the thought of taking any other route?

Dismissing the feeling she carried on along the wider path, her thoughts focused on reaching the inn. She had taken but twenty steps when she came to an abrupt halt. One glance back over her shoulder made her question her judgement.

The earl lived nearby.

For some strange reason unbeknown to her, she turned around, retraced her steps and hurried down the narrow lane. Instinctively, one knew when something felt right. The further down the lane she ran, the more at ease she felt with her decision.

Doubt surfaced when she came to the clearing and stumbled upon the huge, rusty iron gates. A large imposing Elizabethan building stood at the end of the path—the home of the Earl of Hale, she presumed.

The gates were locked.

With a thick chain wrapped around the railings, it was impossible to open them. Judging by the number of weeds sprouting out of the gravel, the entrance had not been used for some time. The impression was one of neglect, of desolation, of utter hopelessness.

Evelyn was not foolish enough to climb the gates, and the stone wall running along the boundary seemed too high.

No doubt there was another way in.

She followed the boundary until she came to a tree; its lowest branch overhung the wall. Bunching her dress to her knees she climbed up, receiving a few bumps and grazes in the process. If only she'd not discarded her blood-stained gloves, she thought, as she lay along the branch and pulled herself across before jumping down into the earl's estate.

When she eventually reached the oak front door, it was dusk. With no sign of activity, she glanced at the twenty-or-so windows scattered across the facade. Not a single light shone from within. Each one looked dark and ominous, conjured an image of its master's disfigured face lurking in the shadows.

Evelyn wrapped her cold fingers around the iron knocker and let it fall. The dull echo resonated along the hallway beyond. She waited for the clip of footsteps, for the rattle of keys, for any sign someone was home.

Nothing.

Determined to raise a response, she knocked again, twice.

Nothing.

"Damn it all." The curse burst from her lips. Her aunt lay bleeding to death, the coachman a lifeless lump. She'd run until her chest burned, until fire scorched the back of her throat. She'd fought her way in, her hands battered and bruised, her cloak in tatters.

The earl would welcome her even if she had to pound on the door until her fingers bled.

Racing to the lower level window, she cupped her hands to her face and peered inside. Seeing nothing but the eerie outline of a suit of armour she moved to the next window, and the next, until she'd worked her way around to the west wing.

When she looked through another window, she noted the fire blazing. The bright orange flames roared within the stone surround to illuminate the room.

She saw him then—the maimed earl.

He sat in a wingback chair, wearing a fine shirt and waist-coat, his head bowed as he stared into the flames. A mop of ebony hair hung over his brow. His hunched shoulders reflected his melancholic mood.

Evelyn rapped on the glass pane, but he simply sat there as cold and as solid as a block of stone.

An elderly woman entered the room. Her stout frame and apron suggested she was a housekeeper or cook.

Evelyn tapped again. "Please, I need your help. Please let me in."

The woman caught her gaze and muttered to the gentleman in the chair. She pointed to the window and then threw her hands up in the air.

Without raising his head, the earl waved her away, refused to look at her let alone listen to her plea.

"Please!" Evelyn banged the window with both fists.

The woman shrugged and left the room.

Evelyn turned away in frustration, paced back and forth while she decided what to do. She should have taken the other path. She would have been at the inn by now. She would have found help.

Why wouldn't he open the door?

Did he think she'd be appalled by his face?

Frustration turned to anger when she thought about her poor aunt, and she kicked the gravel along the walkway.

Then she saw the stone. Smooth and oval, it was small enough to fit in her palm, large enough for what she needed.

Before rational thought found its way into her muddled mind, she picked it up and hurled it at the window.

The sound of shattering glass accompanied the earl's deep masculine curse.

CHAPTER 3

*A*lexander shot out of the chair, his gaze fixed on the smooth stone lying amidst the shards of broken glass. Thankfully, the windows were striped with lead, and only the bottom pane had shattered.

Mrs. Shaw came scurrying in, wiping her hands on her apron. "I heard a noise, my lord. Is everything all right?" Her eyes widened when she looked to the window. "For all the saints, what on earth …"

The lady stood outside, her hand plastered across her mouth.

Alexander inhaled.

He could smell her blood, just a hint, fresh and sweet.

Swinging round, he turned his back to the window. "Get rid of her. Get rid of her now."

Mrs. Shaw gasped. "But she might be hurt, my lord, she might need—"

"I don't care what she needs." And he didn't. Other people's petty trials were no concern of his. "Drag her away kicking and screaming if you have to. Just get rid of her … and find out how the hell she got in."

Pacing back and forth to stop his traitorous mind from considering any other option, he clenched his teeth and hardened his jaw.

She was probably just another ogler come to see the hideous earl. He knew what they called him. Perhaps she thought he needed saving. Perhaps she needed money and preferred to lie with an ugly man than to suffer the pain of hunger writhing in her belly.

The thought of hunger roused the faintest flicker of sympathy.

Something forced him to turn back to the window: a tug in his chest, in his abdomen—but the lady was gone. A sense of relief coursed through him, accompanied by the familiar feeling of regret.

Ignoring the broken glass scattered about the floor, he threw himself down into the leather chair and resumed the state of thoughtful contemplation as he continued to gaze into the flames.

He heard the lady's cries and protests resonate along the hall as Mrs. Shaw met her at the front door.

"Wait, wait, you can't come in. His lordship doesn't take kindly to visitors."

"Do I look as though I'm here to take tea?"

Alexander straightened. The predator in him was alert and ready to pounce—the man curious and inquisitive.

"Come back here. Trust me. You won't want to make him angry."

"Do I look as though I care? I have far more important things to worry about."

With those blunt words, the lady burst in through the door, forcing him to jump up from his seat and face her while Mrs. Shaw waddled in behind.

"I tried to stop her, my lord. I told her you don't want company."

He raised a hand to calm his housekeeper.

The lady strode up to him, coming to a halt a mere foot away. She wore no bonnet. Her chestnut-brown hair looked dull and shabby. Her left cheek was grazed, the skin red and swollen, the rest of her face smudged with dirt. Her filthy cloak did not look fit for a pauper. Yet in spite of it all, her countenance conveyed strength, good breeding and an unshakable resolve.

"You must hurry," she said, not bothering with an introduction. "There's been an accident … my aunt is … my aunt is—"

She stopped abruptly, her curious gaze searching his face as though scrutinising every line, every detail. He knew why, of course.

She had been expecting a monster.

"Your face," she continued, tilting her head. "There's … there's not a mark on it. Not even a blemish."

He couldn't help but smirk.

With a look of wonder, her gloveless hand drifted up towards his cheek, and he noticed her dirty nails and the cut that ran across one knuckle. Worst of all, he noticed the dried blood.

Sucking in a breath, he stepped back.

"Forgive me," she said, dropping her hand and shaking her head. "I don't know what came over me. I heard you were … that you were—"

"Disfigured."

"That you'd been in an accident and had suffered—" She gasped, and her hand flew to her chest. "The accident! Our carriage has overturned, no more than a mile from here. My aunt has received an injury to her head. I need your help. Please, you must come quickly."

Alexander shook his head. He could not be alone with

her, not in the forest at night, not when there would be blood. "I'm afraid I cannot help you."

Her mouth fell open.

"There's an inn a few miles along the road," he added, not knowing why he felt a sudden need to offer assistance. "My groom will escort you there directly. I suggest you leave now. It will not take long to prepare the horses."

"But there's no time. It will be too late. You must come now."

"I can't help you."

She turned away from him and muttered something about taking the wrong path. Hitting her clenched fists against her legs in protest, she swung back around. "Do you have kin, my lord? Do you have someone you care for, someone you would do anything to save?"

"I have no one." The words were not said to incite pity, and anger flared when her gaze softened.

Mrs. Shaw gave a weak smile and shuffled further back into the shadows.

The lady stared at him. "Well, there must have been someone once, someone you cared for?"

Alexander considered the question. He'd had a mother who lavished gifts and attention on her lovers, a father who appeared indifferent and a whole host of women he'd barely even liked.

"No," he repeated, aware his tone sounded cold.

"Oh. I see. Well, I have one person who means the world to me, and she is lying in an upturned carriage, teetering on the brink of death."

Alexander knew how it felt to waver between the two worlds, to feel the icy pull of death sucking him under while he struggled to cling to life.

"I would do anything to save her," she continued.

"As I said, my groom will escort you to the inn. You'll find a—"

"Why won't you help me?" Her eyes brimmed with tears, and he could feel her frustration. "Outwardly, you may not look like the beast everyone believes you to be. But a man with no heart surely hides a monster within."

She looked shocked upon uttering the words, and his attention was drawn to the full lips responsible for forming them. If only she knew the truth lurking within her statement. It was the beast inside he was trying so desperately to keep at bay.

Refusing to accept his decision, she thrust her arm out and grabbed his sleeve. "Please, I implore you, my lord. You must help me."

The touch of her innocent fingers caused the fire in his blood to rage. But it felt different. The urge to drink from her, to feel the thick, warm liquid coat his tongue and throat was tempered by another feeling—an obscure need to comfort and protect.

It rocked him to his core.

In the last two years, he had never felt anything close, most human emotions being a distant memory. So why now? Why this particular lady? Perhaps he had not lost everything after all. Perhaps his humanity was still trapped inside the body of a beast, waiting to be released, waiting for an opportunity to reveal itself.

If he let this lady leave, he would never know.

"Very well," he suddenly said, driven by an overwhelming desire to test the theory. "I will see what I can do."

The lady gave a relieved gasp, which was nothing compared to Mrs. Shaw's shocked expression as she hovered in the background.

"You will wait here while—"

17

"But I will need to show you where to go. It's dark out. You'll never find your way."

Alexander did not need her help. He would have no problem following the scent of blood or the smell of death.

"I move too quickly. You will never keep up."

"I will."

"You'll be a hindrance."

"I won't."

"Stay here." It was an order not a request, and he ignored her forlorn expression to take a few strides towards the door.

She rushed to his side and placed her dainty hand on his thin linen sleeve. "Please, my lord. What if it's the last time I'll see my aunt alive? What if I miss the chance to say goodbye?"

Alexander should have felt indifferent to her exaggerated display of sentiment, yet something deep inside him stirred. He could not argue with her logic or motive, and he found he admired her persistence.

If only someone had fought for him with such passion. If only someone had thought him worth saving.

"If you fall behind, I will continue without you." His words were deliberately blunt, harsh even. "We will need to cut through the forest on foot. It can be treacherous enough by day."

She raised the hem of her gown a fraction to reveal a pair of sturdy brown boots and then gave a satisfied grin. "These will suffice."

Mrs. Shaw stepped forward. "I'll pack water, bandages, a needle and thread. Come, miss, you can wait for the master in the kitchen."

Five minutes later, Alexander strode out of the herb garden, through the alley of overgrown topiary to the door in the boundary wall, aware that his quarry tottered behind him in a bid to keep up.

He stopped as his hand curled around the iron ring on the door. "I'll be quicker on my own," he said, offering her one more chance to change her mind.

"I'm coming with you."

The wooden door scraped along the ground as he forced it open and he raised the lantern to light their way.

"Be careful where you place your feet and stay close behind. If you fall, I won't carry you."

They made their way through the forest, the crunching and cracking underfoot breaking the uncomfortable silence. She failed to suppress a groan when she almost stumbled, and he resisted the urge to offer assistance.

"How did you get in?" He asked the question purely to prevent his solitude from being disturbed by another unwelcome intruder.

"The gate was locked," she said, pausing to catch her breath, "so … so I climbed a tree and dropped down over the wall."

"Wearing a dress?"

"I had no other choice."

"How did you know where to come?"

"My aunt said the Earl of Hale lived nearby. I assume you're him."

"I am." Or he had been once. Now he was but a fragment of his old self.

No doubt her aunt was the one who had told her the tale of his scarred face, and she had come to the house expecting to be greeted by a monster. The lady certainly had courage in abundance.

"Wait," she said, and he swung around to find her leaning back against a tree trunk, her hand covering her heart. "I think … I think we're going the wrong way."

Alexander lifted the lantern higher, purely for effect. "No, we're not." He imagined her inquisitive mind trying to establish how he knew the way. Her aunt must have lost a fair amount of blood as the potent smell hung in the air, drawing him closer. "It's this way."

She stared at him, her silver-blue eyes peering through the darkness like bright stars in the night sky.

"You said the gate was locked," he continued by way of an explanation. "Therefore, you took the lane at the fork in the road. I doubt you're capable of running more than a mile, so I have a reasonable idea where I'm going."

She raised her chin in acknowledgement, and they continued through the forest. Despite snagging her dress on bracken and dead branches, she kept moving, radiating a level of determination he found admirable.

When they found themselves out on the road, she barged past him and stopped in the middle of the path. With her hands on her hips, she searched left and right. Eventually, she pointed to the left and said, "It's this way."

She didn't wait for him but lifted her gown an inch and ran through the darkness, her torn cloak billowing behind her. Alexander followed, choosing to hang back rather than race on ahead.

"I think that's the carriage," she said, calling to him over her shoulder as a monstrous shadow appeared in view. "Aunt Beatrice. I'm here."

The carriage lay on its side, but there was no sign of the horses or the coachman. The lady tried to climb the wreckage in an attempt to reach her relative.

"Here, let me try," he said, tugging at her cloak for fear of touching her.

She stepped down and took the lantern. "Quick. You must hurry."

He grabbed the spokes of the wheel and vaulted up before dropping down inside the conveyance.

"Is she all right? Tell me she's alive! Tell me all is well."

"At least give me a minute to look," he shouted with some frustration.

Alexander placed his fingers to the woman's neck. "She's alive." Even so, her pulse was weak, and she had yet to regain consciousness. He ignored the blood, the sight causing a painful pang deep in his belly. Rolling the woman into his arms, he stood and lifted her closer to his chest, shuffling her up over his shoulder so he could use his hands to climb out.

It was not an easy task.

"You're going to drop her."

"I am not going to drop her. If you're so worried why don't you put the lantern down and help me, damn it."

"There is no need to curse and shout. I am only ..."

Her attention was drawn away, and he followed her gaze to the cart clattering into view further along the road.

Without a word, she ran forward and held the lantern aloft. "Stop, please we need your help."

There were two men in the cart, one being the innkeeper, Fred Harlow, and the other he assumed was their coachman.

The cart stopped directly in front of them, and the men jumped out.

"I'm sorry, miss, for going off and leaving her," the other man said. "I took the horses and went to get help."

Fred Harlow came up to the carriage. "Do you need help, my lord?" he said, failing to hide his surprise.

"If you could take her arms, I think that would be best. We'll lay her down in your cart so we can treat the wound to her head."

"Right you are, my lord."

The men carried the old woman to the cart and used a stuffed sack as a pillow while Alexander examined the cut. "It will need a few stitches before you can take her anywhere. Hopefully, after a few days' rest, she'll be up on her feet."

When no one volunteered for the task, he turned to the lady. "What's your name?"

"My name?"

"I assume you have one."

"It's … it's Miss Bromwell."

"Miss Bromwell, you will climb into the cart and hold your aunt's hand while I stitch her head. If she wakes and is startled, I fear I shall do more damage."

"Do you even know what to do?" she said as she climbed up and crouched next to him.

"Would I attempt it if I didn't?"

"Have you done this sort of thing before?"

"Many times."

She sighed when she looked at the old woman, took the ghostly pale hand and brought it to her lips. "Don't leave me, Aunt Bea. Don't leave me here alone."

Alexander swallowed. The overpowering scent of blood made it more difficult for him to concentrate, and the odd feeling in the pit of his stomach sent his thoughts into disarray.

"Just hold her still while I sew." The quicker he got on with it, the quicker he would be rid of them.

Miss Bromwell ignored his harsh tone and sat through the whole procedure without looking away once. She continued to stroke the woman's hand and whisper endearments while he covered the wound with a bandage.

Alexander glanced at the innkeeper. "There, all done. Take it steady on the way back. You'll need two to lift her into bed."

Fred Harlow shook his head. "There's no room at the inn for them tonight. What with the cockfight in Brier's field, and the road closed near Setley, we're having to put 'em up in the barn."

Alexander jumped down and pulled the man to one side.

"I'm sure you will find somewhere suitable. I shall make it worth your while."

Fred threw his hands up. "You can't expect me to drag folk from their beds at this hour. Their coachman says they're on their way to Mytton Grange. If you send word, I'm sure they'll come and take 'em off your hands."

Alexander gave his most stern frown. "Are you saying you won't help me?"

"What can I do? I've already given up my own bed." Fred sighed. He stared into Alexander's eyes and then said, "I suppose I could see if anyone minds sharing."

"That won't be necessary," Miss Bromwell said, coming to stand at his side. "The Earl of Hale could not possibly allow gently bred ladies to stay at an inn full of cockfighters. I'm sure he will be most happy to shelter us for this evening and on the morrow we shall send word to Mr. Sutherby."

"Mr. Sutherby?" Alexander enquired. "Who the blazes is Mr. Sutherby?"

Miss Bromwell straightened her back and raised her chin. "Mr. Sutherby lives at Mytton Grange, a well-kept house a few miles from here. He is extremely sociable and well-mannered and will welcome us with open arms."

There was no mistaking the veiled insult. "He sounds like a perfect gentleman."

"He is the very best of gentlemen. Mr. Sutherby is to be my betrothed."

CHAPTER 4

*E*velyn could not decide if the Earl of Hale despised her, despised women or despised people in general.

He was rude, conceited and almost always angry. No wonder they made up stories about him being so hideous. Outwardly, his clear complexion revealed a strong, handsome face. His steel-blue eyes were captivating; his dimpled chin suggested a playful charm. Inwardly, he was the most abhorrent gentleman she'd ever had the misfortune to meet.

Thankfully, Mrs. Shaw demonstrated a level of hospitality one expected from her master and had brought a bowl of broth to her aunt's room. The woman still hovered in the background while Evelyn attempted to feed her aunt a spoonful of the vegetable soup.

"I have never seen her look so pale."

"I wouldn't worry, miss. The master knows what he's doing, and if he says she'll be right in a day or two, you can be sure of it."

"At least one of us has faith in him," Evelyn said, not bothering to hide her disdain.

Mrs. Shaw shuffled forward. "I know he's not an easy

gentleman to converse with. I know he seems a little sharp, a little brash at times—"

"Brash? He is downright rude."

"He doesn't take kindly to visitors that's all."

"Well, he's in luck. I doubt he's likely to receive any when he behaves like such a heathen."

The Earl of Hale had refused to ride back to his estate, Stony Cross, in the cart. Evelyn had sat and watched him stalk off through the forest, baffled by his constant sour mood. By the time they'd reached the old house, and a servant had come down to unlock the gate, the earl was already home hiding in his study.

They had received no welcome or assistance from the earl, no offer of food or hot water to bathe—nothing.

"It's complicated," the housekeeper said cryptically. "He's not what he seems."

The woman's loyalty knew no bounds, which she supposed was a rather endearing quality.

Evelyn placed the bowl on the table next to the bed. "People seldom are what they portray." She walked over to the washstand, wrung out a cloth and came back to wipe her aunt's cheeks.

"Why don't you leave her to rest? You could do with a wash and something to eat. There's water in your room next door though it'll be a little cool now."

At the mere thought of food, Evelyn's stomach gurgled in response. "What if something happens while I'm away?"

"She just needs rest. I'll look in every ten minutes or so to check on her. Besides, you're no good to her like that. She'll need you fit and healthy."

Evelyn nodded. "I suppose you're right. I'll wash and then nip back in for five minutes."

Mrs. Shaw smiled. "Come and find me in the kitchen when you're done."

Evelyn spent ten minutes staring at her reflection in the mirror. The bruise on her cheek would take more than a week to heal, and she would still be finding knots in her hair come June.

After scrubbing at the dirt and soaking her hands, she went to work on brushing out her hair. She must have spent an age on the task and Mrs. Shaw knocked to see if she still wanted supper.

"Do you have any spare pins?" Evelyn asked. "So I can put up my hair."

"There's no one here who'd use such things." Mrs. Shaw scanned Evelyn's loose hair, a smile touching the corners of her lips. "There's no one here to fuss neither, so you can come down as you are."

Mrs. Shaw led her downstairs, to the room with the broken window, which had since been temporarily repaired with a piece of wood. "You sit here in front of the fire and get warm, and I'll bring your supper to you."

Despite the golden glow cast from the fire and an array of candles, the room felt dark and oppressive. It was like walking into Lucifer's inner sanctum, and she peered about the room expecting to find the disagreeable earl lurking somewhere in the shadows. Thankfully, she was alone. And so she settled into the wingback chair, removed her boots and tucked her feet under her legs.

Mrs. Shaw brought in a simple platter of meat, cheese and bread. Either the earl had reduced the monthly allowance, or he'd insisted the guests were not to be spoilt. Perhaps he feared they would try to prolong their stay, and he would be forced to be civil. Grateful for even the smallest morsel, Evelyn tucked in.

"Would you like more logs on the fire?" Mrs. Shaw said, placing a glass of wine on the low table in front of the chair.

Evelyn looked up at her in surprise, wondering if the earl

knew his housekeeper had raided his cellar. "No, I'm quite warm. Thank you for the wine."

"You're welcome, miss. Well, I'd best go and check on your aunt."

With that, the woman left her to her meal.

Despite the warmth radiating from the hearth and feeling content after supper, Evelyn still struggled to relax. The wine helped, the full-bodied claret was rich and soothing, and she curled up in the chair as her lids grew heavy. It wouldn't hurt to take a little nap. Not after the stressful events of the day.

Had she known she would dream of the earl, she would have taken a needle and thread and sewn her eyelids to her brow.

No one could predict their dreams. Some dreams were dominated by a series of images, often fragmented, yet richly vivid. In this dream, she was still sitting in the chair, aware that the earl was in the room. Yet she could not see him as everything appeared to be black.

She felt his presence beside her, felt him take a lock of her hair between his fingers, heard him inhale. She felt his gaze drift over her face and body, leaving a warm trail in its wake. Then the soft pads of his fingers stroked her cheek with a level of tenderness she did not expect from such an odious being. When his thumb caressed the line of her lips, she woke with a start.

The gentleman responsible for her racing pulse was sitting in the chair opposite, his gaze dark and brooding as he stared at her over the rim of his wine glass.

"You're sitting in my chair."

Evelyn tried not to look flustered, but she felt hot, breathless. "You ... you had no trouble finding another."

"If you want to sleep, you have a room upstairs."

A blush rose to her cheeks at the thought of him watching her in slumber. Why hadn't he called Mrs. Shaw to wake her?

Why had he stayed to watch? Probably to annoy her or give him a justifiable cause to complain.

"I was not sleeping. I was simply resting my eyes."

He snorted and cradled the glass closer to his chest. The light from the floor-standing candelabra cast a glow over the deep-red liquid. "It is the same thing."

"I'm sure you would argue with me no matter what I said."

He took a sip from the glass, his gaze never leaving her. "Perhaps."

Evelyn refused to be intimidated by his penetrating stare. What did it matter if he was mean and abrupt? There was a much more considerate man residing a few miles away. "I shall need to send word to Mytton Grange. Mr. Sutherby is expecting us."

"Ah, Mr. Sutherby, your perfect gentleman. It has been taken care of. I expect his reply first thing."

The conversation felt awkward, the atmosphere tense. He gave nothing of himself—no hint of warmth or emotion, no clue to the man hidden beneath the austere facade. In his desperation to be rid of her, he'd already written to Mr. Sutherby. This may well be the last time she would see the Earl of Hale and the thought gave her the courage to be bold.

"Well, I shall certainly be glad to leave. I have never spent time in the company of a gentleman so rude and unfeeling."

"Unfeeling?" he said with a snort. "Did I not save your aunt from death's door? Was I not the one who stitched the wound?"

Evelyn was still baffled as to why such a cold man had taken the trouble. "I'm certain your motives were purely selfish."

The earl sat forward. "How so?"

"Because you wanted to be rid of me and thought it the

quickest way, or for some other reason I have not quite fathomed."

"You're right on both counts. I do want rid of you, for reasons I do not care to go into."

Evelyn gasped at his blunt reply. The man had no care for the feelings of others.

"What happened to you, to make you like this?" she said, waving her hand at him.

He took a long, slow sip of wine and licked the residue from his lips. "You would not believe me even if I told you." His gaze drifted past her shoulder to stare into the distance, and she thought she saw pain and anguish reflected there. After a moment, he shook his head and said, "Has Mr. Sutherby made you an offer of marriage?"

Why on earth should she divulge anything about herself when he insisted on being so insular? But she felt the need to fill the uncomfortable moments of silence, and when she spoke, she forgot her heart was pounding.

"He has broached the subject with my aunt and made it clear that is his intention. I believe he will ask me tomorrow when I meet his sister." The weird feeling surfaced again at the thought: a prickling sensation irritating her shoulders, causing her to shiver.

"But you're not sure you want to accept. You're struggling with what you think you should say and what you want to say."

Evelyn's mouth fell open at such an insightful response. She snapped it shut. Were her feelings so obvious to others? If the earl could see the truth, then so would Mr. Sutherby.

"Mr. Sutherby is a handsome, kind and generous man," she said. "A lady would be foolish not to admire such qualities."

The earl narrowed his gaze. "But there is something missing, something more that you want."

"What more is there?"

He stretched out his legs and crossed them at the ankles. "Oh, I think you know."

"If I knew, I would not have asked the question."

"Because you have suppressed your true feelings. Tell me. Tell me what you really want." His gaze became more intense, more focused, his voice a seductive whisper that sent tingles through her body. "Tell me what it is you dream of when you're alone at night. Tell me. Tell me now."

Evelyn felt the heat building in her stomach, making a slow ascent, filling her chest. She felt lightheaded and giddy, the aftereffects of too much wine. The warmth flooding her body banished all of her fears and concerns, and her thoughts were filled with dreams of love. She found she could not keep the words at bay. Now the dam was open, a torrent of suppressed emotions rushed to the fore.

Tell me.

The words echoed through her mind, dragging a confession from her lips.

"I … I dream of a man who loves me above all else," she began, feeling suddenly light and free as if she were floating. "I dream of a love so deep I would rather die than live without it. I long to feel the physical ache only true love brings. I dream of a man who is my friend, my companion, my lover. A man whose touch soothes my soul and ignites a passion—"

"Enough," he said, his voice firm, commanding. "Enough."

Tiny white lights flashed before her eyes, and she blinked rapidly as the heat ravaging her body subsided. When her vision cleared, he was watching her, his sinful gaze penetrating her soul.

"Sorry, what was I saying?" she asked, her mind still addled.

"You said Mr. Sutherby was handsome and kind but that you don't love him."

Evelyn put her hand to her throat as if the action would somehow eradicate the words. "I ... I did not say that. I did not say anything about love."

"Yes, you did. You believe Mr. Sutherby falls short of your expectations."

"Are you deliberately trying to provoke me?" she said, shooting up out of the chair, gripping the arm to steady her balance. She did not want to accept the truth in his words. It was easier to carry on pretending everything would work out fine, to pretend she could learn to love a good man. What was there not to love? "Are you so eager to be rid of me that you would call me a liar?"

His gaze swept over her. "Do not be dramatic."

She knew she was overreacting, but the need to stamp her doubts and worries into the ground surpassed all else. "If you insist on arguing with me, I am going up to bed."

"Do you think running away will solve your problem?"

"Perhaps I'm tired, tired of listening to advice from a man who barely lives in the real world, a man so cold and detached he may as well be dead."

Evelyn slapped her hand across her mouth, shocked at her disrespectful outburst. All this talk of Mr. Sutherby had left her nerves in tatters, and the earl had a way of bringing out the worst in her.

The earl did not look offended. He simply raised his glass in salute. "Then sleep well, Miss Bromwell. I have a feeling tomorrow will be a rather interesting day."

CHAPTER 5

*E*velyn gave a disgruntled sigh, plumped her pillow and cuddled into it. Sleep often eluded her. Her mind always chose the early hours to mull over the day's events. And the day had certainly given her a tremendous amount to contemplate.

Although she was loath to admit it, the earl was right. She did not love Mr. Sutherby.

It was a complicated dilemma.

Was it silly and naive to imagine one must love a man with all of their heart before agreeing to a lifelong commitment? Then again, perhaps marriage was the solid foundation needed for feelings to blossom and grow into the sort of love that lasts forever. Of course, it helped if the gentleman was kind, well-mannered and polite.

Her thoughts were drawn to the earl. His dark, oppressive mood made her angry, made her feel frustrated and confused as she struggled to understand him. Yet he had managed to peer into her soul as if it were an open window. One glance and he knew the fears and doubts hidden inside. Mr. Sutherby did fall short of her expectations. She didn't love him. And there *was* a vital ingredient missing.

Damn the earl for interfering.

Damn him for being so perceptive.

Feeling the need to find a distraction she climbed out of bed, rummaged through her luggage—the small trunk having been retrieved from the wreckage—and put on her wrapper. There was not much she could do in the middle of the night. But she'd sit and comfort her aunt who, despite being weak and lethargic, had regained consciousness.

The earl had been right about that, too.

Evelyn eased the door away from the jamb and crept out. For some reason, she stepped left instead of right, lured by the moonlight streaming through the window at the end of the hall. She'd spent many a sleepless night staring up at the moon. The vision created a stillness within, a feeling she belonged to something infinitely bigger, and it made her feel at peace.

Her feet carried her to the window before her mind conjured the thought, and she drank in the sight of the silver sphere set against the inky-black sky. Lost in thoughtful contemplation, she didn't notice the earl at first. He stepped off the gravel path and walked towards what would have once been a decorative garden. The overgrown topiary spilt out onto the path, the water no longer flowed from the spouts on the fountain and the rose bushes were scraggy and unkempt.

Where could he be going at such an ungodly hour?

With no warning, he swung around and punched the air. Evelyn jumped back into the shadows for fear of being seen. Had his anger reached such an uncontrollable level that he was forced to take his frustration outdoors?

Curiosity burning away inside, she edged back to the window and peeked out. She saw the earl sitting on a bench opposite the fountain. He was staring up at the moon as though the Lord had forsaken him and he was pleading for forgiveness; then he looked down and cradled his head in his hands.

Good Lord!

Was he weeping?

A lump formed in Evelyn's throat; a hollow cavern opened up in her chest. She fought the powerful urge to go to him, to ease his troubled mind, to find the good buried so deeply within. Struggling with a range of surprising emotions, she closed her eyes to calm the restlessness consuming her.

When she opened them again and found the courage to look out, she was not prepared for the shocking sight that greeted her.

The earl had removed his coat and cravat and was busy stripping off every other piece of clothing until he stood naked, bare as the day he was born. Beneath the celestial setting, his skin glistened with a silvery sheen. His muscular body was carved to perfection: powerful, hard, yet graceful. Even though she knew it was wrong—a gross invasion of his privacy—she could not help but stare in awe at the sculptured contours.

The Earl of Hale was a magnificent specimen of a man.

With an open mouth, she watched him walk down to the bottom of the garden, to the narrow river meandering through his property. Without hesitation, he slid into the water and out of sight.

Evelyn didn't make it to her aunt's room.

Instead, she threw off her wrapper, climbed into bed and pulled the sheets up to her chin, all in a desperate bid to dampen the fire burning in her belly. She could not erase the image from her mind.

Never in her life had she known a man be so bold, so unconventional, so exciting.

How was it possible to despise a man and desire him both at the same time?

A strange need clawed away at her, and she plastered her hand over her mouth to help ease the shock. Half of her wanted to throw on her clothes and run as far away from Stony Cross as her legs could manage. The other half wanted to strip off everything and swim naked with him in the river.

Oh, God!

She thrust her head under the pillow as a way of shutting out the world, and after dismissing an array of lascivious images, involving firm buttocks and well-developed thighs, she finally fell asleep.

"Wake up, miss, wake up. It's ten o'clock."

Mrs. Shaw shook the bed with such force she thought she might fall out. Evelyn groaned and turned over in protest. How could it be ten? She felt as though she'd only been asleep for an hour.

"You need to get up. A letter has come from Mytton Grange."

It took a moment for the words to penetrate and Evelyn opened her eyes as the thought echoed in her mind. She should have been ecstatic. She should have been clambering over the bed in a rush to get to her clothes.

"Is … is Mr. Sutherby sending his carriage?"

Why did she have the overwhelming feeling that she did not want to leave? Why had she developed a sudden affinity for the place?

"I've left the letter in his lordship's study. He won't be down yet."

No, Evelyn thought, probably because he had spent the night boxing an invisible opponent and swimming naked in the river.

"How's Aunt Beatrice this morning?"

35

"Much better," Mrs. Shaw said with a smile. "She has managed to eat a bit of toast."

The sense of relief caused her to sigh loudly. "I'll wash and dress and spend some time with her before I eat. Do you think she will be fit to travel?"

"I'm sure she will. It's only a couple of miles and she can rest when she gets there."

"Oh."

Mrs. Shaw poured fresh water into the pitcher. "I'll be sad to see you go. It's been nice having someone to talk to."

The thought of leaving caused another pang of sadness in Evelyn's chest. How odd.

"You have been very kind, Mrs. Shaw. I'm sure I would have been left cold, filthy and starving if it wasn't for you."

Mrs. Shaw gave a weak smile. "Oh, his lordship would have mellowed, eventually. He's a good man deep down. Never forget that."

Evelyn didn't see the earl at breakfast, although it was almost twelve when her growling stomach forced her to leave her aunt and go in search of food. There was no sign of him when she wandered through the house. There was no sign of him in the garden when she examined the fountain and sat on the bench. The same bench where he had so shamelessly discarded his clothes.

A frisson of excitement raced through her at the thought.

When the rain came, she rushed inside and almost collided with Mrs. Shaw.

"His lordship said to tell you that Mr. Sutherby will be calling later today. You're to make sure your things are packed and waiting in the hall."

Obviously, the earl couldn't wait to be rid of her. Anger flared. All of these conflicting emotions were giving her a headache.

"Could he not come and tell me so himself?" she said

loudly in the hope he would hear her. "It is not as though he could offend me any more than he has already. He has made it clear he wants us out of here as soon as possible."

Mrs. Shaw bent her head and whispered, "It's more that he doesn't want to become acquainted with Mr. Sutherby, for fear the gentleman will call in when he's passing. I'd prepare yourself. I expect his lordship will be blunt and rather unkind."

His lordship's mood did not concern her; she had grown quite used to it in the few hours she'd spent with him. But she refused to be ignored or treated with contempt. He should have consulted her regarding any arrangements made.

"Where is the earl?"

Mrs. Shaw glanced to the closed door at the end of the hall. "In the study … but you can't go in there. No one's allowed in there."

Evelyn marched to the door and knocked.

There was no reply.

"He doesn't like to be disturbed," Mrs. Shaw said with a look of panic. "Not so early in the day."

Evelyn shrugged. "He doesn't give a hoot for the feelings of others. Why should I give a hoot for his?"

Before she could change her mind, Evelyn gripped the handle and burst into the room, despite Mrs. Shaw tugging at the sleeve of her dress.

The earl was not sitting behind his desk, and Evelyn froze in shock as she studied the dimly lit room.

The walls were lined with dark oak panels, the wooden shutters pulled across to block out the light. The timbered ceiling made the room feel small, confined. In the corner, a warm glow radiated from the tall candelabra even though it was the middle of the day.

"What the hell are you doing in here?" His deep thunderous roar emanated from behind the door. Like a frightened animal, Mrs. Shaw retreated into the hallway.

Evelyn refused to let fear quash her anger. She slammed the door shut to find the earl sitting on a stool in front of an easel.

"Get out!" He jumped up to block her view, knocking over the stool in the process.

Stand strong, she thought, remembering Mrs. Shaw's words that he was a good man beneath the bravado.

Evelyn squared her shoulders. "I am not leaving until you pay me the respect I deserve."

He stepped forward, his large frame towering above her, his jaw clenched. But she recalled the image of the sad gentleman sitting on the bench. She recalled the image of a man struggling to suppress his pain.

"If you want rid of me, you will have to pick me up and throw me out," she continued, swallowing down her nerves.

He straightened. "Are you refusing to abide by my request?"

"I am." Evelyn folded her arms across her chest to reinforce her position.

Uncertainty flashed in his eyes. He was obviously used to people doing what they were told. "Then you leave me no option. I will simply drag you out."

"No, you won't. You may be rude and odious, but you would never hurt me."

Evelyn had no idea what he was capable of, but she would take a chance. His sharp tone did not worry her anymore. She moved to the desk, pulled out the chair and sat down.

"I would like you to tell me what arrangements have been made for me and my aunt."

He hovered near the easel, his hesitant feet moving to step

forward before stopping. "Wait out in the hall, and I will find the letter."

"I am waiting here."

He muttered a curse and thrust his hand through his hair. "Are you always so stubborn?"

Evelyn smiled. "Only when the need arises."

As another curse left his lips, he stomped over to the desk, rifled through his papers and practically threw the note at her. "Here. You can read it outside."

Evelyn ignored him. She unfolded the paper and read the missive. Mr. Sutherby had expressed his concern for their welfare and asked to call for them at two. A hollow feeling gripped her as it was almost two o'clock. Soon, she would be far away from Stony Cross and the sour-faced Earl of Hale, never to cast sight on either of them again.

As though reading her thoughts, the earl said, "I told him he could call at five."

"But I thought you were desperate to be rid of us," she said, wondering what had prompted the change of heart.

"Five o'clock suits me better."

"Of course," Evelyn replied with a snort.

He jerked his head towards the door. "Now you have seen the note you can go."

It occurred to her that his rudeness was a mask for something else. What was he hiding? What was he scared of? That strange feeling swamped her again: the need to soothe his wounds, the need to hear kind words fall from his lips.

Evelyn stood, and he looked relieved. But rather than head for the door, she walked over to the shutters.

"Why is it so dark in here?" she asked, determined to unnerve him. "Why does it feel as though someone has died, and the house is in a constant state of mourning?"

She touched the shutters, and he gasped, rushing over and patting them to check they were still in place. With his mind preoccupied with the shutters, she strode over to the easel to examine his sketch in the hope it would reveal something of the man he kept hidden.

The sight caused all the air to leave her lungs. Her heart skipped a beat as a rush of pure emotion exploded until her eyes brimmed with tears.

The Earl of Hale had sketched the most beautiful portrait of her. She was sitting on the bank of a river filled with water lilies, the reflection of the moon shimmering on its mirrored surface. She wore a sleeveless dress, her hair cascading in ripples over bare shoulders. He'd captured her unusually wide eyes to perfection, although her lips appeared fuller, more sensual. There was something magical about the scene, something ethereal.

Evelyn swung around to look at him but could find no words to express the strange feeling that consumed her.

The earl stood and stared in a moment of frozen stasis, yet she sensed his embarrassment. For the first time since meeting him, she thought she saw something more than frustration and irritation flashing in his eyes.

She had no notion how long they stood in stupefied silence, staring deep into each other's eyes. But a loud rap on the door broke the spell.

The door opened a fraction, and Mrs. Shaw popped her head around. "Forgive me, my lord, but Mr. Sutherby has arrived."

His anger surfaced immediately. "Well, he can bloody well wait. I told him to come at five. Is the man so stupid he cannot read?"

"I've put them in the drawing room. What with it being so overcast today, it will be the most suitable place."

"Them?"

"The gentleman's brought his sister with him."

The earl dragged the palm of his hand down his face and cursed again. "We'll be along in a moment."

Mrs. Shaw left them, and the earl nodded to the easel. "I often sketch when I've nothing else better to do," he said, his tone frosty.

Evelyn suppressed a smile. Nothing he could say could demean the effort it had taken to capture her likeness or the fact that he had chosen her as his subject. This tortured, complicated man was certainly an enigma.

Evelyn walked towards the door. She stopped in front of him and placed her hand lightly on his sleeve. "It's beautiful," she whispered. "So beautiful it makes me want to cry."

He swallowed visibly before replacing his mask of indifference. "I'm not the sort who enjoys displays of sentimentality. But rest assured, the kindest, most handsome man in all of England has come to your rescue."

Evelyn pulled her hand away, but the frisson of excitement the connection stirred still coursed through her body. "People are not always what they seem, my lord," she said. "I have heard it said that the coldest of men often hide the biggest heart."

"That is where you are wrong, Miss Bromwell. The coldest men often have no heart."

CHAPTER 6

*E*velyn's heart pounded in her chest as she walked across the hall towards the drawing room. The inevitable day had come. The day when she would have to confront her feelings for Mr. Sutherby. Yet she suspected the rapid beating had more to do with the earl's hot palm on her back as he guided her towards the room. Even when his hand fell to his side, she could feel the imprint searing her skin like a branding iron.

"My dear, Miss Bromwell." Mr. Sutherby jumped from his seat as though the padding was on fire. His mop of fair hair flopped forward as he rushed to grasp her hands. He brought them to his mouth and brushed his clammy lips across her bare skin. "You look so weak, so frightfully pale. What a horrendous time you've had. We've been so worried, haven't we, Charlotte?"

"Indeed, we have hardly slept a wink," said the golden-haired beauty coming to stand at his side.

Dressed impeccably in a fashionable fawn silk gown and tucker, Charlotte Sutherby made Evelyn feel positively frumpish in her plain muslin dress. Vanity was a trait she despised yet she suddenly wished she'd spent more time on her appearance.

"Allow me to introduce my sister, Charlotte." Mr. Sutherby gestured to the lady as she offered a demure curtsy.

"It is a pleasure to meet you, Miss Sutherby," Evelyn said. "If only our first meeting could have been under less harrowing circumstances."

"When we heard what had happened to you, Miss Bromwell, we were aghast," Charlotte said, clutching her hands to her chest.

Evelyn could feel the earl's penetrating gaze boring into her back. Hostility hung in the air like a guillotine, waiting for the opportune moment to come crashing down on its victim.

"Please, you must call me Evelyn," she said, dismissing the earl's sudden intake of breath. "Allow me to introduce you both to our generous host, the Earl of Hale."

The Sutherby siblings' respectful greeting was met with a frown severe enough to silence a pack of howling dogs.

"When I gave instructions to call at five, I meant it," the earl said sharply. "I cannot abide shoddy manners."

Mr. Sutherby's sky-blue eyes flashed with surprise.

Miss Sutherby's mouth opened and closed a few times before she stepped forward. "Surely you can forgive this one misdemeanour, my lord." She batted her lashes in such a salacious manner that Evelyn felt a tiny stab of jealousy upon anticipating the earl's excited reaction.

"No, I'm afraid I cannot," he said, oblivious to the woman's charms. "When I invite someone to my home, I expect them to pay me the respect of arriving on time."

Mrs. Shaw was right. The earl seemed determined to ensure they never called upon him again.

Rather than challenge the earl by using the unfortunate accident as an excuse, Mr. Sutherby offered his usual affable smile. "You're right. Forgive our rudeness, my lord. It will not happen again."

The earl inclined his head in response. "I should think not, as you shall have no need to call again."

An uncomfortable silence ensued, and Evelyn turned to the earl and whispered through gritted teeth, "Are you going to offer them tea?"

He shrugged in response. "I do not drink tea," he said loud enough for them to hear. "This is not a social call. It is the only reason I have let them stay."

Evelyn waited for Mr. Sutherby to challenge the earl for his coarse manner and for showing his sister such disrespect. But the man said nothing. Timidity was not a quality she desired in anyone, let alone a man destined to be her husband. No lady could possibly be happy on the arm of a coward.

"There is no need to be so rude," Evelyn said, determined to defend them. "You know why they're here. And I'm certain they have no intention of ever daring to turn up uninvited."

His gaze searched her face and his mouth curled up in response. "Then they may sit while Mrs. Shaw prepares your aunt for the journey."

Mr. Sutherby should have told him to go to the devil. He should have stormed out to wait for her in his carriage. Instead, both brother and sister sat down near the window and conversed about the appalling weather. Evelyn sat with them and relayed details of the accident while the earl sat in the farthest corner of the room, hidden in the shadows.

Evelyn tried to concentrate on the conversation, but her attention was drawn to the brooding figure in the corner. Surprisingly, she found she preferred his scathing honesty to Mr. Sutherby's placid temperament. The gentlemen were equally handsome. However, the earl's features were more rugged, more intriguing, reflecting the mysteriousness of the night, as opposed to Mr. Sutherby's sunny disposition.

You don't love him.

The words drifted through her mind without provocation. No matter how hard she tried she could not dismiss them. Whenever Mr. Sutherby spoke, they popped into her head again, and she felt relieved when Mrs. Shaw entered to inform them her aunt was ready to depart.

Their luggage had been loaded, and Aunt Beatrice helped up into the carriage. The Sutherbys thanked the earl for his hospitality. But his cold reply sent them scurrying into their conveyance like mice fleeing a cat's claws.

"Thank you for helping my aunt," Evelyn said. The earl refused to see her to the door, and so they hung back in the dark hallway. "I'm sorry if I made you feel that you had no other choice."

"I do not dwell on the past. It is done with, forgotten." He stepped closer, took her chin between his thumb and forefinger and stared into her eyes. "You may despise my blunt approach, but honesty delivers a short, sharp blow. To live a lie causes a constant pain that lasts a lifetime. Remember those words when you listen to what your kind, affable gentleman has to say."

How did he know what she was thinking? How was he so perceptive to her needs? How was he able to see into her soul and understand her fears and doubts? She had an urge to reach out to him, too, to offer comfort. But she wouldn't know where to begin.

Without another word—without a parting greeting or a promise to meet again—he dropped his hand and walked away from her. His sudden absence created an empty feeling she could not explain.

Mrs. Shaw was standing near the carriage door, waiting to wave them off. "Now, you mind how you go," she said. "I've packed a tincture for your aunt that should help take down the swelling. Just a spoonful before bed should suffice, and she'll be as sturdy as a butcher's block in no time."

Evelyn hugged the old woman. "He's lucky to have you," she said, nodding towards the house. "I can't thank you enough for all you've done for us."

Mrs. Shaw batted Evelyn's arm. "You'll make an old woman sob on the doorstep if you carry on like that."

Evelyn smiled and moved to open the carriage door. She stopped and turned back to the housekeeper. "I know his title, but what's his name? He never told us, and he is not the sort of man one asks."

Mrs. Shaw returned her smile and then peeked back over her shoulder. "It's Alexander Cole."

Alexander Cole.

The name sounded familiar. A warm feeling flooded her chest as she repeated the words. She wondered what it would be like to be on such intimate terms with him his given name would fall gently from her lips.

Evelyn glanced up at the array of windows covering the facade. She sensed his presence lingering in the shadows but saw nothing. Despite everything he said and did, she felt comfortable at Stony Cross. Her mind was engaged with fanciful notions of tending the garden, restoring it to its former glory. In her dreams, the sound of laughter and gaiety would echo through the cold, dark passages. Alexander Cole would smile not frown.

With a loud snort, she shook her head. Perhaps the accident had left her brain swollen, too tender. Perhaps she was desperately trying to cling on to any other thought rather than one involving her betrothal to Mr. Sutherby.

Alexander stood away from the window. As he listened to the sound of the carriage rattling down the drive, he tried to come to terms with the range of conflicting emotions plaguing him.

The first, most shocking discovery was that he wanted Miss Bromwell to stay.

Perhaps it had something to do with his mistrust of the Sutherbys. They appeared exactly as Miss Bromwell described: kind, friendly and well-mannered. Yet he had picked up threads of their thoughts, small fragments of feeling suggesting a discord between their words and their motives. In that respect, Charlotte Sutherby reminded him of the golden-haired devil who had lured him away from the tavern. Even when Miss Sutherby flashed a coy smile and attempted to soothe him with her pretty eyes, he felt disdain burn in his belly.

He felt the same way about her brother. He could not imagine the fiery-tempered Miss Bromwell being happy with a man like Mr. Sutherby. Maybe it was the reason his mind roused murderous thoughts when the gentleman brought Miss Bromwell's bare hands to his lips.

Luckily, he had fed his craving.

Still, he contemplated ripping out their throats with his teeth even though the thought of drinking their tainted blood made him nauseous.

The next surge of emotion occurred when he'd heard her name—Evelyn—though he preferred to think of her as Eve. A daughter of God lured into sin by the Devil's own beast. The thought conjured a series of lascivious images to flood his mind; her soft breasts squashed against his chest, her tongue dancing dangerously with his. Indeed, for the first time in two years, his cock was so hard he almost felt human.

That thought led to another emotion, one far more damning—he cared what happened to her.

It was the only logical conclusion he could draw from the

tight feeling in his chest, from the stone-like lump in his throat. He had thought all human emotions lost to him, buried beneath a solid block of ice. But he'd sensed the cracks appearing, felt the plates shift under his feet.

Perhaps Miss Bromwell was to be his salvation.

Although she truly would despise him when she knew what he was.

Mrs. Shaw's discreet cough disturbed him.

"They've gone, my lord," she said, hovering at his side, "and Peter has followed them down to lock the gates. There'll be no more disturbances."

Alexander turned to face her. He had known the woman his whole life. From her pursed lips he knew there was something she wanted to say.

"You may say what you will, but do not expect a reply."

She took a deep breath. "I know you fear being in company, but you've spent a day with Miss Bromwell and survived. I'm sure if you started going about in society you could control your urges."

"*She* survived, you mean. I did not ravage her neck and drain her blood."

In Miss Bromwell's company, he found his human emotions suppressed the animalistic appetite that clawed away at him. It would not be the case with others.

"One day is not enough time to make a calculated decision," he continued. "I would rather a life of solitude than live with something I regret."

"Why don't you call at Mytton Grange and spend an hour with them? I'm sure—"

"I'm not spending another minute with the Sutherbys." He could feel his rage returning.

"You'd have the perfect excuse as you could say you're checking on Miss Bromwell and her aunt."

"And what would you have me say when they offer tea? That I prefer something darker, thicker?"

"Miss Bromwell liked you," she added with a hint of desperation in her tone.

"No, she didn't. She thought me rude, arrogant and brash."

Mrs. Shaw did not argue with his assessment. "Well, I still think you should go and check on her. That's what a gentleman would do."

Alexander put his hand on his stomach to show his displeasure at her comment. "That was a low blow. I ceased being a gentleman two years ago, as you well know. Next, you'll be telling me to grow up and be a man. Well, how can I when I'm a bloody monster?"

He had lost everything that night in Bavaria. The memory was akin to a crippling disease ravaging his body, each visit gnawing away at all that was left of the man he remembered.

"I didn't mean it like that," Mrs. Shaw said, her face flushing.

Anger and resentment surged up to breach the surface. "Just leave me the hell alone," he said, striding from the room. Crossing the hall to his study, he slammed the door to stress his point.

Years of frustration always found an opportunity for release. His housekeeper knew to ignore his temper; she knew not to take offence at his churlish manner.

He flung himself into the chair, let out an exasperated growl loud enough to rattle the shutters, before closing his eyes. When he opened them, his gaze flew to the sketch of Evelyn Bromwell. Jumping up, he charged over to the easel and ripped the paper from the wooden clamp. The urge to tear it to shreds almost overtook the need to treasure it, to preserve it.

He didn't need to be reminded of his humanity, of all that he had lost.

But what if the tenderness expressed in her face was the only thing creating the warmth in his chest?

What if he couldn't recapture the likeness?

Alexander moved towards the desk, unlocked the top drawer and with careful fingers placed the sketch inside. Even after he'd locked it and relaxed back in the chair, Evelyn Bromwell continued to haunt his thoughts.

A strange sense of foreboding fell over him when he thought of her alone with Mr. Sutherby. Perhaps he could wait until nightfall and wander over to Mytton Grange. It would not be a social call. An hour or so hiding outside would give him an opportunity to study the situation, to discover if Evelyn Bromwell had accepted the hand of such an insipid gentleman. He may even uncover what secrets the Sutherbys were hiding.

CHAPTER 7

*W*hen the mantel clock struck nine, Alexander's impatience could no longer be tempered. Since deciding to investigate the Sutherbys' house, he had struggled to focus on anything else. Indeed, his constant pacing had created a clean pathway on the dusty floor.

Mytton Grange was a manor house situated two miles north of Stony Cross. There were no tenant cottages, the owner having sold them when he moved to Italy.

The quickest route took Alexander down to the fork at the end of the lane, to follow the road leading past the coaching inn before branching back up through the forest. The stone bridge crossing the river was in dire need of repair, but he navigated his way across the crumbling arch before climbing the stile bordering the manor.

The wind had settled. The night was dry, the sky clear.

Drawn to the orange glow emanating from the tall window, he crossed the grass and peered inside to find Miss Bromwell, Mr. Sutherby and his sister seated around the fire.

A smoky haze hung in the room, and Alexander plastered

his back to the wall when Mr. Sutherby darted over to the window and yanked up the sash.

"I'll have a boy climb the chimney." Sutherby coughed before sucking in the fresh air. "You'd have thought the agent would have cleaned them out."

Recalling Sutherby's mass of golden hair, Alexander imagined shoving the gentleman up there in the hope the soot choked him.

"I'll find some water," Miss Bromwell said. He identified her assertive tone with ease. "It's best we put the fire out before the whole stack goes up in flames."

When she left the room, Charlotte Sutherby came to stand near the window and said with some impatience, "Well, have you asked her?"

Mr. Sutherby sighed. "No. I've not had a chance. When I asked to speak to her alone, she made an excuse about needing to settle her aunt. I get the sense she's avoiding me."

"Perhaps she's ill. She hardly ate a thing at dinner. It can't be anything else. She seemed quite taken with you when we were in London."

"What if we made a mistake in coming here?"

"You needed to place a little distance between you. It wouldn't do to make it too easy. Besides, a well-kept house such as this speaks volumes when one is considering marriage."

Alexander suppressed a snort. If that were true, there wasn't a woman in all of Christendom who'd consent to marry him.

"We'll discuss it later," Miss Sutherby continued as the door opened and Miss Bromwell returned. "What a gem you are, Evelyn, you've found Thomas. Throw the whole bucket on the fire, Thomas, before we're smothered in a thick blanket of smoke."

Alexander heard the flames crackle and sizzle in protest.

"Let us vacate this room," Mr. Sutherby said. "We could retire to the library, and you could read to us, Charlotte."

"Shall I light the fire in the library, sir?"

"No, no. Best not light a thing until they've all been swept. And I suggest you leave this window open for an hour or two."

"Forgive me," Miss Bromwell interjected, and he could hear the nervous hitch in her voice. He should have insisted they stay at Stony Cross. He should never have let her leave with Sutherby. "I think I will retire for the evening. It has been a long day, and I still feel exhausted after the accident."

"Surely you'll not leave me alone to listen to Charlotte's ramblings?"

"Ramblings! I have just the right tone to recite poetry," Miss Sutherby said. "But perhaps we should all retire. There'll be plenty of time for conversation tomorrow. Indeed, we could take Evelyn riding and pack a picnic. You do ride, Miss Bromwell?"

"I do, although—"

"Excellent. Do you hear, Nicholas? We shall all ride out together tomorrow."

When Miss Bromwell left the room, Alexander expected the Sutherbys to follow, but they hung back. They'd moved from the window, and so he strained to listen to the rest of their conversation.

"Must I do everything for you?" Miss Sutherby snapped. "Thanks to my intervention, you will have a few hours alone with Miss Bromwell. I shall feign a twisted ankle, making it impossible for me to accompany you on your picnic. It should be plenty of time to secure her hand."

"What if she refuses?"

"Then you must persuade her. It's not as though she's had a better offer. And you are deliciously handsome."

"You're biased. Perhaps the earl has shown an interest in

her. You saw the way she looked at him. They've obviously met before as she was far too comfortable in his presence. She didn't even flinch at his rudeness."

"Don't be ridiculous. Miss Bromwell is a darling, and the Earl of Hale is an ogre. The two do not go together."

Alexander could not disagree with her statement. He was vastly more terrifying than she could ever imagine.

"Come, let us go to bed," Miss Sutherby continued. "There is a lot to do tomorrow and a good night's sleep will do wonders."

They left the room. Alexander slid down the wall into a sitting position while he contemplated what he had heard.

Mr. Sutherby appeared a little more than desperate to press his suit. And his sister was prepared to do her utmost to help. For some inexplicable reason, Alexander felt a frisson of pleasure at the thought of Miss Bromwell's reluctance to hear the fop's declaration.

Something about the whole situation bothered him. Frustrated that he had not picked up the same conflicting feelings he had experienced earlier in the day, he brushed his hands through his hair and looked up at the moon.

At night, he felt normal.

At night, he was no different from other men.

He was drawn to the moonlight like others were drawn to sunlight. It relaxed him. It made the world come alive. The daylight had been taken from him, whipped from under his feet with one sinister bite and he'd been left to roam a world of darkness, lost to the night for all eternity.

Feeling a sudden need to return to the sanctuary of his home, he stood and made to depart. The shadowy figure moving furtively across the lawn rendered him frozen to the spot. The strides were purposeful, quick, determined. The woman, for she was too petite to be a man, knew where she was going.

It was Evelyn Bromwell.

He knew it like he knew his own name.

Where the hell was she going wearing nothing but a flimsy dress, and so late at night? Was she on her way to meet a beau for a midnight rendezvous? Was that the real reason for avoiding a conversation with Mr. Sutherby?

Hiking up the hem of her skirt, she climbed the stile, glancing once over her shoulder but failing to see him cloaked in the shadows. Curiosity burning in his belly, he made a stealth-like pursuit to avoid detection, cowering behind bushes and darting behind a tree trunk.

When she reached the river, she stopped and scanned her surroundings before placing her hands on her hips as she looked up to the heavens. The moon appeared larger, brighter. Its reflection slithered over the surface of the water. It called out to him, and he resisted the urge to reveal himself, to strip naked and plunge into the icy depths.

Under the light of the moon, he felt free.

He felt like he belonged.

In an uncharacteristic moment of madness, Miss Bromwell suddenly stretched out her arms and twirled round and round, her loose chestnut hair billowing out until dizziness caused her to stumble.

Alexander moved to step forward, the desire to join her in her frolicking suppressed by the need to offer assistance. But Miss Bromwell just giggled, giving him a moment to think of a logical reason to explain his presence.

However, all logical thought escaped him when Miss Bromwell fumbled with the buttons on her dress.

In the stillness of the night, he could feel the blood pumping through his veins; he could hear it ringing in his ears. Excitement, coupled with an intense rush of anticipation, were emotions he had not experienced for such a long time—even in his human form he had been cold and detached. Now the feelings swamped him, forced him to watch though he knew it was wrong.

A wave of white muslin shimmied to the ground, pooling around her feet. She wore no corset or excessive petticoats, just a simple chemise.

Alexander's cock pulsed at the sight of her curvaceous outline, and he almost burst out of his breeches when the garment joined the puddle of discarded material.

Bloody hell!

Miss Bromwell stood a few feet away from him, the sight of her deliciously round derriere causing him to moisten his lips. Her skin had an incandescent sheen, a silvery essence that shimmered with a magical quality amidst the woodland setting.

What was he to do now?

He could hardly step out from behind the shrubbery. A gentleman should turn away and make a hasty retreat, the need to respect her privacy being the prime motivation.

But Alexander was no gentleman.

Evelyn moved to the river's edge and dipped her toe into the murky water. Good heavens, it was so much colder than she expected, but she refused to turn back now.

When she'd climbed the stairs to bed, it had not been her intention to strip naked and splash about in the river. But she'd spotted the moon shining brightly in the night sky, and her thoughts had drifted back to Alexander Cole.

No matter how hard she tried, she struggled to understand him. The cold, cynical manner he portrayed was so opposed to the man who had sketched such a pretty portrait. Even his parting comment, where he had explained the folly of living a lie, suggested a deeper level of concern for her welfare.

That was why she had come outside, to understand what motivated him, to understand the lure of swimming naked on a moonlit night.

Finding the courage to continue, she sat on the bank and slid slowly into the water, clutching onto a grassy mound as she had no idea of the river's depth. Luckily, it only came to her elbow. She shivered as she walked out into the middle and the cold water lapped around her waist. Holding her body rigid and her arms tucked into her sides, she ducked down until it covered her shoulders, suppressing the urge to curse as loud as she could.

The freezing water penetrated her bones, making her skin tingle as the blood pumped rapidly around her body in protest. She thought it best to keep moving and so swam a few strokes towards the opposite side.

"Is Mr. Sutherby so lax in his hospitality he has failed to provide water to wash?"

Startled by the sudden intrusion, she tried to stand up, splashing water over her face as she lost her balance.

"Who … who's there?" She turned and almost shot up out of the water when she noticed the gentleman sitting on the bank. Remembering she was naked, she clutched her arms to her chest as a way of preserving her modesty.

With her mind quickly thawing from the shock, the arrogant tone struck a chord of familiarity. "Lord Hale? Is it you?"

He stood and moved to the water's edge. "I was passing and thought you had fallen in."

She felt a flush rise until her cheeks burned. "But … but you live miles away."

"I often walk at night. I suggest you keep moving else you'll catch your death. I'll wait here in case you get into any difficulty. Unless you want me to help you out." He bent down and offered his hand.

"No!"

"You complained about my hospitality. At least I provided warm water to bathe."

"You're not funny. As I recall, it was Mrs. Shaw who tended to our needs."

The earl seemed different, less angry, less agitated. He sat on the grass. "Please, continue with your ablutions. I shall just wait here."

"Go away," she cried, her temper overshadowing her embarrassment. "I cannot get out while you're sitting there gaping."

"Then you should have thought of that before stripping off your clothes, eager to partake in a midnight swim."

What a hypocrite!

"And you never feel the urge to partake in such things, my lord?"

He gave an indolent wave. "Do I look like a man who enjoys swimming in cold water?"

She ducked down and waved her arms about in a bid to keep warm. "What, you have never stripped off all of your clothes and left them on a bench near a fountain? You have never swum naked in the middle of the night?"

It was too dark to gauge his reaction fully. After a brief silence, he said, "You saw me?"

Evelyn gave a satisfied smile. "I saw everything. I'm afraid I struggle to sleep and often wander about at night." As she spoke, her teeth began to chatter, and her limbs grew stiff. "I need to get out before I'm struck down with cramp."

"I'm not stopping you. After your declaration, I think it only courteous you allow me to watch."

What had happened to him in the few hours since she'd left? She much preferred bantering with this gentleman than arguing with the moody earl. "You surprise me, my lord. I did not think the word *courteous* was part of your repertoire. Now turn around while I get out. And no peeking."

Evelyn swam to the bank.

"I've seen plenty of naked women. One more won't make a difference."

"I'm sure you have. Now turn around."

He sighed, stood up and turned his back to her.

Placing her palms on the bank, Evelyn tried to push herself up. Damn. She appeared to have lost all the strength in her arms, and her legs felt numb, too.

"With all the huffing and puffing, I assume you're struggling to get out. Perhaps now you will thank me for waiting."

"Just give me a minute."

She tried again but slipped back into the water.

"Would you like a hand?"

"No."

"Then how do you propose to get out?"

Weary from the effort, Evelyn conceded. What other choice was there? "Very well. Give me your hand. But close your eyes."

He came closer to the water's edge, offered his hand and closed his eyes. With no option but to trust him, she placed her palm in his.

That one innocent touch sent her world spinning into a tizzy of raw emotion. The tingling radiating from his palm shot up her arm, flooded her chest, forced her to gulp a breath.

With brute strength, he pulled her out. When her feet were safely on the grass verge, she stood and stared at him. With his eyes closed he looked so peaceful, so breathtakingly handsome, yet his ragged breathing revealed an inner frustration. Still gripping her hand tightly, he opened his eyes. But he did not glance down.

The look of longing she saw there made her heart ache.

Her nakedness was a mere trifle compared to the intimate way he was able to strip away the barriers to reach her soul.

She closed her eyes for her own protection. They were a gateway he could easily access. When he pulled his hand away, she opened them to see him stride over to the trees.

"Get dressed," he barked over his shoulder, anger evident in his tone.

Evelyn was not offended by his sudden coldness. She could feel his torment, feel his fear. A connection had grown between them, a familiarity too complicated to define.

Fear engulfed her, too.

How could she consider a proposal from Mr. Sutherby when her mind was so muddled? How could she consent to be another man's wife when she could think of nothing other than Alexander Cole?

CHAPTER 8

*N*othing could erase the past. Nothing could change what he had become. That's the thought he replayed over in his head while he waited for Miss Bromwell to dress.

Yet he could not fight the instant connection he'd felt upon taking her hand. Or shake the feeling that their paths were destined to cross. Perhaps it was a form of punishment? He had seduced many women, not caring for any of them. Why should he care now when his condition made it impossible for him to act?

Punishment was the wrong word. It was torture.

Alone and sheltered, he could have taken Evelyn Bromwell. He could have drunk from her, drove into her hard and deep, over and over, made her forget it had ever happened.

A beast would have done exactly that. Yet he could not behave like the animal he had fought so hard to suppress. Besides, there was something more to this frisson of excitement he experienced upon seeing her. An inexplicable need to look beyond carnal pleasures in the hope of finding a richer treasure.

Feeling her presence at his shoulder, he turned and scanned the dishevelled sight.

"I'd pray Mr. Sutherby doesn't see you like that else he'll be retracting his offer."

She brushed the stringy tendrils back off her shoulders and pulled at her dress as the fabric clung to her damp body. "He hasn't made me an offer, not yet."

"I'm sure it is only a matter of time," he replied, not wishing to reveal what he'd heard. "I'll walk you back to the house in case you faint from exposure to the cold and get eaten alive by squirrels."

She chuckled. "Squirrels?"

"The area is overrun with them," he replied without raising a smile. Although when she glanced nervously over her shoulder, he had to purse his lips.

He chose not to help her over the stile. To touch her again would be a mistake and he could feel her assessing gaze drifting over his face.

"You didn't tell me what you were doing out here," she said, "and before you say anything, I do not believe you were out walking."

After preaching about the wisdom of telling the truth, he had no option but to be honest. "I came to spy on the Sutherbys. I don't like them. They are so affable they make me want to spew on my boots."

She chuckled again. "There is nothing wrong with kindness. Perhaps you should try it."

"It is overrated. Besides, was not my rescuing you from a freezing river an act of kindness?"

"I suppose so. But why are you so concerned about disliking the Sutherbys? I thought you disliked everyone."

"Not everyone," he said, glancing down at her. "I like Mrs. Shaw."

Miss Bromwell smiled. "You're lucky to have her. I don't know how she puts up with your vile moods and tantrums."

He knew how lucky he was. The old woman had been an angel at a time of desperate need. When he had eventually found his way home to Stony Cross, she knew instinctively all was not well with him. It had nothing to do with his filthy clothes and unkempt hair. He'd fallen into her arms and sobbed. It hadn't taken much to confess his sins, to explain the thirst that controlled him. She had stood by him, would never abandon him, despite his faults and weaknesses.

As they approached the house, he thought he saw the shadow of a figure in the upstairs window.

"I'll leave you here," he said, not wanting to alert anyone to his presence. "Next time you go swimming in ice-cold water, I suggest you find a place where someone can hear your cry for help."

When he turned to walk away, she called out to him. "Do you think you'll be out walking tomorrow night? Will you come to spy on the Sutherbys again?"

There was no mistaking the warmth in her tone. She wanted to see him, and the thought brought a slight sliver of hope. "That sounds like an invitation, Miss Bromwell."

She struggled to look at him. "Make of it what you will."

He did not know what to make of it, and so inclined his head and bid her goodnight before marching off across the lawn. He would be a fool to meet with her again.

But then he'd been a fool most of his life.

The next day passed in a whirlwind. Alexander spent most of his time secluded in his study, sketching, thinking. Feeling. He'd recounted the events of the previous night so many times his head felt as though it was filled with lead.

Just when he'd decided not to return to Mytton Grange, a voice in his ear reminded him there were too many coincidences to ignore. Miss Bromwell struggled to sleep at night. She enjoyed swimming naked in the moonlight. Well, she hadn't really enjoyed the experience, but she would if she swam with him. She was the only person he knew who ignored his temper, the only person capable of banishing the feeling of utter hopelessness.

When wallowing in his selfish mood, he imagined relieving the physical ache that consumed him. In creating such lurid fantasies, he convinced himself she could heal his affliction—that he would one day walk the earth as a mortal man.

Consequently, the need to understand this power she had over him, coupled with the desire to dissuade her from making a mistake with Mr. Sutherby, was the driving force behind his decision.

At nine o'clock he set out for Mytton Grange. Would Miss Bromwell be waiting for him? Would she have made her excuses to her host? Or during a leisurely picnic had Mr. Sutherby won her affections?

Alexander spent the rest of the walk trying to pretend he didn't care, and felt relieved when he crossed the bridge, as he was done with thinking.

As with everything in life, there were positive aspects to negative situations. The predator inside made him more attuned to his surroundings, being able to gauge residual imprints of thoughts and feelings long after an event. The more profound the initial feeling, the easier it was to tune into it.

When he climbed the stile and crossed the grass, he was hit by a sudden wave of panic. His mind sensed chaos, desperation. His head shot up in the direction of the house, and he broke into a jog as the need to discover the source of such anguish gripped him.

Although the hour was late, he expected to see the faint glow of candlelight radiating from one of the many windows dotted over the facade. But the house sat in darkness. He raced around the perimeter, peered through every window hoping to spot a sign of life. But the house was as desolate as his forsaken heart.

The carriage house and stable block were also deserted, yet he examined the stalls and scoured the shadows for clues as to their whereabouts. As Alexander exited the block, he caught sight of someone creeping out of a building at the far end.

"You. Wait there!"

Upon hearing Alexander's cry, the figure rushed towards the stone entrance, tripping over his feet and landing face down on the cobbles beneath the arch. Alexander caught up with him and yanked him up by his collar.

"I didn't mean no 'arm," the man cried, dropping the leather bridle to the ground as though it was burning his hands. "I was just taking it for cleaning that's all. I was gonna bring it back."

"I'm not interested in what you're doing. I want to know where I can find Mr. Sutherby." Alexander released the man as a gesture of goodwill. "Don't think of running."

The man gulped as he surveyed the breadth of Alexander's chest. "He's gone. They've all gone, gone to London first thing this mornin'."

"London? Why?"

"I don't know." The man shrugged. "All I know is, he let us all go without notice and he ain't even paid us since he's been 'ere."

"When you say all of you, do you mean the stable hands?"

"All the help. Even the housekeeper. Sent all the horses back to Mr. Blake, too."

Plagued once more by a strange sense of foreboding, Alexander tried to shake it. "Did Sutherby say when he'd be back?"

"When we begged him to keep us on, he said he wouldn't be comin' back. Not ever."

What the hell had prompted such an action?

"The blighter borrowed a collection of poetry books that hold great sentimental value," Alexander lied. "If he's bloody well taken them with him, there'll be hell to pay."

"I don't know anythin' about no books. But the door to the kitchen's always left open. If I'm caught in there, I'll face the noose." The man nodded his head towards Alexander's immaculate attire. "Wouldn't hurt if *you* went in and had a look for them."

Alexander bent down and picked up the leather tack, thrusting it back into the man's arms. "You'd better hurry home if you need to give this a polish."

The man's eyes widened. "Thank you, my lord, thank you," he said, grabbing his prize and racing off into the night.

Accessing the kitchen through the herb garden, Alexander moved through the house.

The rooms felt cold, from a lack of personal possessions as opposed to the temperature. Remnants of food, spare plates and cutlery littered the sideboard in the dining room. If he were a servant and had been given his notice, he would not have bothered to clean the place, either.

Sensing nothing to explain their abrupt departure, Alexander climbed the stairs to the bedrooms. A tremor of sexual tension hung in the air, and he burst into the master chamber, his fists clenched, as though expecting to see Mr. Sutherby forcing his attentions on Miss Bromwell.

The room was empty.

The crumpled bed sheets lay strewn across the end of the oak four-poster. Cold, scummy water sat in the washbowl.

The air reeked of masculine sweat. Not the faint acidic scent of poor hygiene but the fresher scent from overexertion. As he rounded the bed, he felt a weird concoction of emotions: desire and love mingled with indifference.

He felt no evidence of panic or fear.

It made no sense.

As he passed the window, he glanced out, noting the perfect view of the lawn and the stile. Had Sutherby seen him with Miss Bromwell? Was jealousy his motivation?

Forcing himself to move to another room, he knew the moment he opened the door that it was Miss Bromwell's chamber. Her presence lingered there, warm, inviting. He could almost hear her chastising him for his vulgar manners, could almost feel the same intense ripples of pleasure he'd felt when his hand touched hers.

Again, he felt no traces of distress, only confusion. It was hardly surprising given Mr. Sutherby's impending proposal.

Perhaps he should have been relieved at her sudden departure. Now, there was no need to spend hours contemplating all the "what if" scenarios. He could return to his simple life, free from obligation.

But dreams possess a magical quality to rise above the mere wishes of men.

Dreams, once embedded into hearts and minds cannot simply be erased or forgotten. Thoughts of Evelyn Bromwell consumed him, as though the essence of the woman had found a way to seep into his blood, into the air he breathed. Despite his best effort, he knew he would not be able to function as he had before. He would not rest until he knew what had prompted the hasty departure, until he knew she was safe and well.

It would mean moving about in Society. If only for a brief time.

The thought forced him to consider what was at risk.

His life would be over if anyone discovered his secret, though this was no life he was living. He was as good as dead. But how would he fare in a room full of people? Could he control the urges? Could he suppress the pangs wringing the muscles tight in his belly? Where would he find the blood he so desperately craved?

Mrs. Shaw would need to accompany him. It would only be for a day or two. Just until he had seen Miss Bromwell. No doubt, he'd stumble upon her and her beau strolling arm in arm through the ballroom. She would regale tales of their upcoming nuptials, her pretty blue eyes sparkling with delight. Anger would bubble away inside, forcing him to be rude.

After all, who would desire a monster when they could have a most affable, kind and handsome gentleman like Mr. Sutherby?

CHAPTER 9

"$\mathcal{J}$t feels so good to be out and about amongst company," Aunt Beatrice said as she adjusted her turban until the feather dangled down over the scar at her temple. "Another day stuck in bed, and I would have started talking to the walls."

Evelyn surveyed the hordes of people crowded into Lord Melbury's ballroom. "Are you sure you wouldn't rather be somewhere quieter? I can make our excuses to Mr. Sutherby. Under the circumstances, I know he would understand. We could—"

"Heavens no," her aunt exclaimed. "You have wasted far too much time tending to me. You need to be out in Society, and then everyone will know of your attachment to Mr. Sutherby."

Evelyn tried to protest but struggled to get a word out. After feeling helpless and being cooped up like a chick in a nest, her aunt was chirping more than usual.

"Besides," Aunt Beatrice continued, "I much prefer the noise and bustle of town. At least there's no danger of being attacked by falling branches. I don't think I'll ever be able to ride through the forest again."

For Evelyn, the opposite was true.

In town, one could not swim naked in the moonlight or be rescued by a dark, brooding gentleman who found pleasure in being rude to everyone he met.

Aunt Beatrice put her fingers to her temple and winced. "Has Mr. Sutherby mentioned the reason behind such an impromptu departure?"

Evelyn shook her head. "Only to reiterate what he told us at Mytton Grange. He had an urgent matter of business to attend to and had no option but to return."

"The man barely gave me time to finish my eggs. I didn't get a chance to crush the shell, and you know what that means—a whole a year of bad luck. In his impatience, I thought he might tear the spoon from my fingers and rap my knuckles." She sighed. "And you know it's not wise to travel on a full stomach. It causes all sorts of problems with my digestion."

No one could have been more shocked at the sudden change of plan than Evelyn.

It was not the distress of having to pack their meagre belongings in a hurry, or the sense of wild panic filling the house, that affected her. Lying awake during the early hours, her mind had been occupied with thoughts of Alexander Cole. Would he walk over to Mytton Grange again? Or would she be left alone in the dark, plagued by disappointment?

Well, she would never know.

The thought caused her throat to constrict.

"Although he has been most attentive to your needs," her aunt continued.

"Who?" Evelyn said. Her aunt couldn't possibly know that the Earl of Hale had rescued her from the icy depths of the river.

"Mr. Sutherby! Honestly, Evelyn, anyone would think you were the one who had injured their head. I said he has been very attentive since our return. I suppose I can forgive him for causing my stomach cramps as he will soon be family."

Evelyn shook her head and glanced over her shoulder. "Shush," she whispered. "He has not offered for me and even if he does, I'm not sure I'll accept."

"What? Of course you'll accept. There's not a man in all of London more suited to you."

Mr. Sutherby had spent the last two days trying to arrange a private meeting and Evelyn had used her aunt's ill health as an excuse. But time had run out. With her aunt's appearance at Lord Melbury's ball, she'd have no choice but to listen to what the gentleman had to say. The thought caused a nervous flutter in her chest that shot up to her throat when she spotted Mr. Sutherby approaching.

"My dear Miss Bromwell, you're looking resplendent this evening," Mr. Sutherby said after bowing gracefully to her aunt. He smiled wide enough to display a full set of white teeth. "Say you'll dance with me. It's been an age since I last twirled you about the floor."

If she danced with Mr Sutherby, it would give her an opportunity to be honest about her feelings. "Of course. I will mark you down for the—" She should have said the waltz, a dance more suited to intimate conversation. "For the cotillion."

Mr. Sutherby inclined his head. "And perhaps you would like to join me in the park tomorrow? Or take a trip to a museum? Charlotte will be happy to accompany us."

Evelyn fell silent for a moment.

"Oh, she would love nothing more, Mr. Sutherby," Aunt Beatrice interjected. "Wouldn't you, Evelyn?"

Before Evelyn could answer, she heard a commotion on

the far side of the ballroom. A sea of heads shot to the door leading out into the hallway. But with the dance floor being overcrowded, she struggled to see what was happening. Sharp gasps and shocked whispers rippled through the room.

"No doubt, someone has fainted from the suffocating heat," Mr. Sutherby said. "Melbury really should limit the number of people he invites to his gatherings."

Aunt Beatrice nodded. "It's only a matter of time before someone …"

Evelyn ignored them, their words lost amidst the strange sensations gripping her. The hairs on her nape tingled. The air around her thrummed with excitement, the vibration causing her breath to come so quick she struggled to swallow.

Eve.

The name drifted through her mind. No one called her Eve, yet she knew it was meant for her. She glanced at Mr. Sutherby and her aunt, who were still discussing the dangers of being trampled in a crush.

Eve.

Despite not knowing who called out to her or where the sound came from, she felt an overwhelming need to respond, albeit silently.

I'm here.

The instant tug hit her deep in her core, drawing her forward, her body moving first while her feet followed. One step became two, and then three as she pushed through the crowd determined to reach the unknown destination.

Around her conversations resumed. The guests regrouped, and the noise of laughter filled the room once again.

Evelyn saw him waiting near the door, ignoring the gapes and stares.

Alexander Cole.

Her hand flew to her heart. It was the only way she could stop it from beating out of her chest.

His dark hair hung in a sinister wave over his brow. His gaze was cold and unforgiving as he scanned the crowd. Wearing full evening dress: a pure white shirt and neckcloth teamed with a black long-tailed coat and breeches, he looked devilishly handsome and downright dangerous. He had the look of a man capable of ripping out another man's heart with his bare hands.

When he saw her, his face remained expressionless. Yet his eyes radiated warmth, the temperature intensifying until the rays penetrated her dress, her skin, every muscle in her body growing limp.

He stepped forward and she waited for him to reach her, fearing her legs would buckle if she moved.

"Miss Bromwell," he said, offering a respectful bow. "You're here."

"Lord Hale." Evelyn curtsied, yet in her mind she imagined throwing her arms around his neck. How bizarre. "Either I am dreaming, or you have left Stony Cross."

"I thought a trip might improve my mood."

Evelyn smiled. "And has it?"

"No. Not until now."

For some reason, she felt her cheeks flame, and she pressed the pads of her fingers to her face expecting to hear them sizzle. "Are you so intent on stalking the Sutherbys that you've followed them all the way to London?" she asked in a bid to disguise the effect his presence was having on her.

The corners of his mouth curved just a fraction. "I am not stalking the Sutherbys. I am here to see you."

Evelyn swallowed as she found his directness oddly stimulating. "And what do you want with me, my lord?"

She was desperate to know the answer, desperate to know what had dragged him from his desolate prison.

"I came to Mytton Grange. It was obvious you'd left in a

73

hurry." He paused briefly. "I wanted to know if you and your aunt were well."

She glanced at the crowd, meeting the shocked expressions on numerous faces. Alexander Cole hated company. He had chained the gates to his estate to keep people out. Yet here he was in a packed ballroom, dressed in his finery, and all because he wanted to see if she was well.

"Why?" The word fell from her lips as she struggled to make sense of it all.

He lowered his head, and she was hit with his musky, masculine scent. "I do not trust Mr. Sutherby."

She reeled from the answer, a rush of disappointment flooding her chest. What had she expected him to say? He was not the sort of man to make false protestations. She was not normally the sort who longed for a gentleman to drop to his knees and declare his affections.

"Then I was correct in my assessment," she said a little coldly. "You are here to stalk the Sutherbys."

He stared at her. His piercing blue eyes searched her face before his gaze drifted beyond her shoulder, and his mouth formed a scowl. "It appears your gentleman has come to claim you."

Evelyn turned to see Mr. Sutherby approach, and she bit back an unladylike curse. "I had come to pay my respects to the Earl of Hale," he said, "but I see he is otherwise engaged."

Evelyn swung back around to see a pair of broad shoulders moving away through the crowd. Damn the man. She would have to speak to him about his annoying habit of walking off before finishing a conversation.

Lifting his chin and tilting his head, Mr. Sutherby continued, "I believe that screech is the call for the cotillion."

Dancing was the last thing on her mind but what choice

did she have? Besides, it would give her a moment to collect her thoughts.

When Mr. Sutherby took her hand, she felt nothing. She could have been holding a dead fish, as even wearing gloves it felt cold and limp. The swapping of partners brought a momentary reprieve. Thank the Lord she'd not agreed to a waltz.

"So what takes your fancy?" Mr. Sutherby asked as they came to meet in the middle of their group.

"My fancy?"

"Tomorrow. Would you rather a stroll in the park or do you desire mental stimulation and would prefer a museum?"

"I … I …"

Mr. Sutherby offered a smile so wide it looked as though someone had sewn the apples of his cheeks to his earlobes and the thread had proved to be far too tight.

"I know. It is a difficult choice. We could always do both."

They rejoined the circle, and Mr. Sutherby pranced away next to her, the shiny buckles on his shoes almost touching his knees.

"I think a stroll in the park," she said, as there would be plenty of people wandering about. Tomorrow, she hoped her mind would be a little clearer. Mr. Sutherby deserved the truth and Evelyn knew she would spend a sleepless night contemplating the dilemma.

"Splendid. I shall call for you at two." He offered his arm as the dance ended. "Come, I shall escort you back to your aunt. Then I shall go and hunt down Charlotte as I am sure she is off causing mischief somewhere."

Aunt Beatrice was engaged in an animated conversation with Mr. Hartwood, whose compassionate nature gave her aunt the opportunity to regale a long-winded account of her dreadful accident.

Evelyn's attention wandered, and she surveyed the crowd looking for Alexander Cole. It took a moment for her to locate him. Now that stories of his disfigurement had proved to be untrue, she expected to find him surrounded by eager guests desperate to know the truth behind the tale.

But he was alone.

Propped up against the wall near the terrace with his arms folded across his chest, he radiated hostility. But like the night she'd seen him sitting on the bench, her heart went out to him. Why she should care about the man was a mystery to her. All she knew was that she wanted to talk to him, to try her damnedest to make him smile.

Perhaps if he explained why he disliked Mr. Sutherby, it might make it easier to reach a decision. Perhaps if she spent more time in his company, it might help her to understand why his voice caused her body to glow, why his touch ignited a fire deep inside.

With that thought in mind, she moved towards him.

CHAPTER 10

*A*lexander could not bear to spend another minute in the packed ballroom. The rank smell of sweat mingled with a trace of vinegar and perfume from those who still wore powder invaded his nostrils. The stench was so potent he only drew shallow breaths.

Besides, he could not watch that fop Sutherby skipping and hopping about the floor again like a hare come breeding season. The fool disappeared through the crowd with Miss Bromwell on his arm, and Alexander clenched his jaw so hard he was in danger of cracking his teeth.

When Alexander entered Melbury's ballroom, he had known what to expect.

People stared at his face, shocked to find no visible sign of the monster hidden within. People whispered and tittered, inventing tales to account for his absence, more tales to account for his attendance. Some dared to approach, eager for the coveted place of being the first to hear his explanation. But one cold, hard stare sent them scurrying back to the hole they'd crawled out of. After an hour, they'd grown tired of watching him, some other on dit taking their fancy.

However, not everyone had lost interest.

He'd noticed the two gentlemen lingering in the alcove. They followed him around the room, hovering in any place that gave them an optimum view. He knew of them. Viscount Markham was the older of the two, perhaps thirty. The Marquess of Hartford, known simply as Devlin, was renowned for his skill with a sword. They met his gaze with an air of arrogance. Alexander's palms itched at the thought of thrusting them both up against the door and wringing their necks.

Needing to find a distraction, he pushed away from the wall and exited through the double doors leading out onto the terrace. The cool night air felt fresh against his face, and he inhaled.

The sound of light footsteps padding across the floor behind him caused him to turn.

"Alexander," Lady Montford breathed softly. "I cannot tell you how pleased I am to see you. I thought you would never return. And then there was that dreadful story about your accident. I've spent two years mourning your handsome face."

His gaze drifted up to the mass of copper curls, down the line of her elegant throat to the exposed curve of her bosom. It was a body he knew well, a body he'd taken many times before.

A body he had no desire to see again.

"How's your husband?" he said, not bothering to hide his contempt. The man spent more time with his horses than he did his wife. Not that she complained.

"Monty? Oh, always away, always busy. You know how it is."

"And your lovers?"

"Satisfying," she replied, trailing her fingers along her collarbone.

"I know you wouldn't accept anything less."

She stepped closer, removed her glove and placed her palm on his chest. "I will push them all out of bed for you, Alexander. It's been so long I've forgotten how good you feel." Her gaze dropped to the fall of his breeches. "Although I've not forgotten how talented you are."

Alexander glanced down at her bare hand. He felt nothing. There was no urgency to claim, no desire to thrust home, no eagerness to give pleasure. His chest felt empty, his cock flaccid.

He stepped away, letting her hand fall. "I'm not the same man you remember." Lady Montford would run for the hills if she knew what he was. It took all his effort not to frighten the conceited grin from her face.

"All the more reason to rekindle what we had. The first time with a new lover is always so exciting. But then we'll have the added bonus of knowing how to please."

Alexander sneered. "I've given up rutting every female I come across. There's something rather tasteless about it."

"Nonsense. Just hearing you say *rutting* has me all aroused. I think you're deliberately teasing me."

Before another word was uttered, Evelyn Bromwell strode out onto the terrace and came to an abrupt halt. Her smile faded as her cheeks flushed crimson and she averted her gaze.

"Forgive me. I … I did not mean to disturb you." She turned and marched back into the ballroom.

"Miss Bromwell, wait."

Lady Montford caught his arm as he set off in pursuit. "Why didn't you say you have a newfound penchant for virgins? I may have tried a different approach."

"Nothing you could say or do would tempt me to accept."

With no time to waste, he ignored the lady at his side and

yanked his arm free. Pushing through the crush, he caught up with Miss Bromwell near the dance floor.

"Miss Bromwell." When she failed to turn around, he grabbed her arm and pulled her back to his chest. "God damn, woman," he whispered through gritted teeth. "Will you wait?"

Upon hearing his curse, she swung around and he released his grip. "It is rude to leave a lady alone on a terrace," she sniped. "I suggest you go back and tend to her needs before someone else does. Besides, I was looking for Mr. Sutherby."

"No. You were looking for me."

Just being in her presence was like drinking a magical elixir. Every part of him thrummed with excitement. Every part of him throbbed, desperate to be near her, to touch her, to lay her down and cover her with his naked body.

"I was not looking for you," she reiterated.

She turned away from him again and pushed through a group of people. When he followed, he realised they were standing amidst the group of dancers, a hundred pairs of eyes focusing on their next move.

Damn it.

Alexander pulled her into his arms, his hand settling on her waist in the hope of joining the other couples dancing the waltz.

"What are you doing?"

"I have no intention of making more of a spectacle than I have already. You will dance with me, Miss Bromwell, and you will damn well smile when you do."

He didn't give a fig what they all thought of him. But he would not have her name sullied. Giving her no other option but to take his hand, he guided her around the floor.

Like a naked flame to a barn full of dry straw, he felt desire ignite so swiftly he almost mistimed his steps. Holy hell, his whole body burned from just the feel of her fingers. He knew that she felt it, too. Her eyes were wide, her lips parted as she struggled to catch her breath. Then the pulsating started. The pleasurable ripples radiated from her palm, shooting into his, running up his arm and down his leg until he felt dizzy.

What the hell was happening to him?

"You feel it, don't you?" she suddenly said. Her ethereal blue eyes were alight with pleasure. "It is like a river of fire flowing through my veins. Tell me what it is."

He shook his head and swallowed hard. "I don't know."

Tiny furrows appeared on her brow. "In my naivety, I thought … well, I imagine this is what desire feels like."

He thought back to all the moments in his life when he had been desperate to bed a woman. He thought back to all the moments when he'd spilt his seed and growled with satisfaction.

"It feels like desire … but something deeper, something different." It was as though they were two halves of one whole. The merest touch reuniting them, bringing them together as it was always destined to be. But he could hardly say that to her. He would keep his damn mouth shut. Those sorts of dreams and whimsical fantasies were not for the likes of him.

"So we both feel it?" she clarified.

Alexander moistened his lips. "Yes, we both feel it, Miss Bromwell."

When he met her gaze, she was staring at his mouth. "If we were alone, would you try to kiss me?" she asked. "I need you to be truthful. I need to understand why I feel this way with you and not with Mr. Sutherby."

At the mere mention of the man's name, the heavenly feeling subsided, and his anger surfaced. "Do we have to discuss Mr. Sutherby?" He had noticed the gentleman watching him twirl her around the floor; his sickly smile replaced with a scowl.

"I'm to walk in the park with him tomorrow, at two."

There was no need to say any more. Mr. Sutherby would make her an offer of marriage, and she would give him her decision.

He glanced at the faint bruise still marring her cheek and the urge to protect her grew fierce. "Do you know what you will say?"

"You were right when you said I don't love him. But marriage is about more than love."

"Is it? To my mind, it should be about nothing else."

Miss Bromwell laughed. "That is easy for you to say. A lady must consider financial support and her husband's ability to provide a secure future."

"Are you saying you would choose stability and wealth over love, Miss Bromwell?"

"No. I'm saying there is more to it than deciding whether you love someone."

"But how do you know Mr. Sutherby is everything he professes to be?" A pang of guilt hit him in the chest. In that regard, he had no right to judge. "For all you know, his mop of hair could be a wig he wears to hide the fact he's bald."

Alexander could not shake his suspicion of Mr. Sutherby. He had been so concerned for Miss Bromwell's safety he'd spent the last two nights trawling about from rout to ball hoping to find her. Numerous hosts had given a disgruntled snort when they noticed him leaving after a few minutes.

"How do I know you're not wearing a wig?" she said with a giggle.

Alexander raised a brow. "You would have seen me take it off when I stripped to go swimming."

Her face flushed, and she bit down on her bottom lip.

"And in answer to your question," he continued, "if we were alone, I would want to kiss you."

Wanting to and doing so were two entirely different things. Once his mouth touched hers, he knew he would struggle to control the urges of the man and the monster.

She gripped his hand a little tighter, and the pulsating returned. "If we were alone, I believe I would allow you to."

It sounded like a challenge, a deliciously tempting challenge. Damn it all, he'd been selfish all of his life. Why couldn't he be selfish now?

"I'm not the sort of man an innocent lady should kiss," he said, trying to dismiss the thought of her moist mouth, of her fingers running through the hair at his nape.

"I know. But are you not the least bit curious? Do you not wonder what this madness is that exists between us?"

Curious was far too mild a word. "Madness? It is an act of lunacy to dream of something that can never be." His gaze dropped to the soft, creamy flesh bulging out of the neckline of her gown and he pressed his tongue to his teeth for fear his fangs might burst from their sheath.

She sucked in a breath. "Yet still you followed me here. Still, you came to Mytton Grange at night, spent hours sketching my likeness."

"I was suffering from a bout of boredom."

"No," she said sharply. "I don't believe you."

He looked down into her eyes. The sense of longing that consumed him was hard to disguise.

The dance came to an end all too quickly, and as he escorted her from the floor, she turned to him. "Will you stroll with me in the garden?" Her words held a hint of desperation that mirrored his thoughts.

He blinked slowly and sighed. "It would not be wise." Sensing a wave of rejection, he added, "You must decide how you feel about Mr. Sutherby. I do not want to influence your decision."

"Are you so confident in your ability to please?" she teased.

He scanned the chestnut curls falling from her coiffure, her full lips and wide blue eyes rousing an image of her swimming naked in the river. Her earthy essence had bewitched him, even on that first night when her cape hung from her shoulders like a tatty rag, her hair a mass of straggly tendrils.

"I am confident in your ability to please, Miss Bromwell."

Before she could respond, they heard a high-pitched cry, and when they pushed through the crowd, Mr. Sutherby rushed to her side.

"Please, Miss Bromwell, I need your help," he said, taking her arm. "Charlotte has fainted, and I cannot rouse her."

"Charlotte? What happened?"

With a look of panic, Miss Bromwell followed Mr. Sutherby to the lifeless figure sprawled out on the floor.

"Please, let Miss Bromwell look at her," Mr. Sutherby said to the group of people congregating around.

As soon as Miss Bromwell knelt down beside the patient, the lady batted her lashes, her lids twitching as she tried to open her eyes. Alexander had never known a person make such a quick recovery. Mr. Sutherby was obviously growing desperate and would resort to any tactic necessary to gain Miss Bromwell's attention.

Miss Bromwell touched the lady's head. "Can you hear me, Miss Sutherby?"

The patient groaned. "Evelyn. Is it you?"

Alexander had never seen such a pathetic display. It didn't matter to him if he stood there all night. Sutherby would not win.

We know what you are.

The words drifted into Alexander's mind, and he swung around so quickly the people behind him jumped back. He scanned the shocked faces, desperate to find the culprit. But his gaze was drawn to the doors leading out to the terrace.

Leo Devlin and Elliot Markham hovered near the exit. The gentlemen were similar in appearance. Elliot's hair was as black as night, cut shorter than the current fashion. It accentuated his firm jaw and gave his face a more rugged appeal. He was taller than Leo Devlin, his shoulders more muscular. Devlin's brown hair hung past his collar, his face holding a more boyish charm. Noticing his scrutiny, both men gave an arrogant smirk before sauntering out into the garden.

He should have left them to their game, but instinct told him to follow. His anger needed an outlet, and he could think of nothing better than wiping the pathetic grins from their faces.

CHAPTER 11

*A*lexander stalked his prey across the lawn, through the maze of box hedges to the orangery. The Gothic structure looked more like a miniature castle than a house for plants. Its parapet walls and stone pinnacles were there purely to support the blanket of arched windows.

Once inside, he followed the gentlemen through the jungle of tropical greenery before stopping at the fountain. Leo Devlin and Elliot Markham were seated on the stone bench, their legs stretched out in front of them, waiting for him to catch up.

"Ah, here he is. The Earl of Hale heard your little gibe, Leo, and by the stern look on his face seeks satisfaction," Elliot said with a smirk.

Alexander turned his attention to Leo Devlin. "What the hell did you mean by it?" It felt good to release some of the hostility he'd spent an hour keeping at bay. He would have the answer to his question.

Devlin raised an arrogant brow. "I meant what I said." He thrust his head forward and whispered, "We know what you are."

Fear clawed away at him, his mind bombarded with images of being bound and dragged out into the daylight to answer for his crimes. The excruciating pain would hold him in its vice-like grip to scorch his soul, to brand him a monster for all eternity.

Alexander opened his mouth to speak, but Elliot stood, his attention moving to a point amidst the exotic trees.

"Shush. Do not say another word," Elliot whispered, tapping his finger on his lips to reinforce his point.

Pushing aside his anger, Alexander listened. The grunts and groans were audible, and he scanned the curtain of dark foliage. Devlin jabbed his finger at a tree, and Elliot sauntered over and disappeared behind it.

"Ah, Lady Conley. How nice to see you again, although I had not bargained on seeing quite so much of you."

Alexander heard a squeal, the rustling of material and a gentleman's muffled protest.

"My dear," Elliot continued, "your husband asked that I find you, for fear you would make him a cuckold again. Now what am I supposed to tell him?"

"Don't tell him," the lady begged. "Please. Don't tell him anything."

"Such a predicament." Elliot sighed. "It is a little too late you see, as there are more witnesses beyond this tree."

"That sounded rather poetic," Devlin shouted. "No doubt the sight of bare breasts has turned your brain to mush."

"I'm afraid I must speak with the lady alone." Elliot stepped around the tree and thrust the gentleman forward. The startled fellow was still busy tucking his manhood back into his breeches as he scurried past them and out into the garden.

"Now, what am I to do with you, Lady Conley?"

The lady gave a long, drawn-out hum. "You … you could take his place. I have always admired you, my lord."

"You mean fill in, so to speak?" Elliot snorted. "I don't think so. It would be like bathing and slopping about in dirty water."

With his anger temporarily forgotten, Alexander pursed his lips to suppress a snigger.

"Well … what about this? Do you think this will help you forget all about it?"

"I might be persuaded."

They heard more rustling, playful giggling, and he noticed Elliot's bare hands grip the scrawny tree trunk.

"Yes, holy hell, you've the tightest mouth."

Devlin glanced at Alexander, gave an amused grin and made a lewd gesture with his hand and mouth. He removed his pocket watch and flicked open the lid. "I wouldn't bother leaving. By the time you reach the door, it will be time to come back. It will all be over in less than a minute."

"I bloody well heard that," Elliot panted. "Oh, God, don't stop."

Elliot's roar of satisfaction announced the end of the lascivious act.

"Told you," Devlin said, flashing the face of his watch at Alexander. "The hand hasn't even moved."

The room fell silent. Elliot stepped out from behind the tree, his face plastered with an arrogant grin as he pulled at the sleeves of his coat and brushed his hand down the front of his breeches.

"Satisfied?" Devlin asked.

"For the moment."

The lady appeared from the foliage, her hair mussed and bedraggled, as though a family of birds had made it their home for the spring. Her lips were red and swollen. Her eyes were glazed with desire.

"You promise to say no more about it?" she said, wiping the corners of her mouth with the tip of her finger.

Elliot nodded. "Indeed."

"And your friends?"

"Consider them mute."

"Perhaps we may stumble on each other again, Lord Markham."

"Perhaps."

"Perhaps not," Devlin joked as the lady closed the door to the orangery and left them alone. "He never touches the same woman twice. It's become a rule of his, and he's quickly running out of options."

"Ah, but I didn't do the touching," Elliot said. He focused his attention on Alexander. "Forgive the interruption. But a starving man never refuses the offer of bread."

Devlin made a puffing sound. "Starving? You have the appetite of an entire pack of wolves. You could have bargained a little harder. You could have thought of your poor friend. I feel as though I've not eaten for weeks."

"It's been a day, Leo. Besides, it wouldn't be fair to leave Lord Hale out."

Devlin threw his hands in the air. "You forget about Eve. A man does not call out in such a mournful way only to fill another woman's mouth an hour later." He jumped up, cupped his hands over his heart and cried, "Eve. Eve. Where are you?"

"I suggest you shut the hell up," Alexander roared, his fists clenched at his sides ready to pummel the smirk off his face. He had been so busy listening to their comical banter he'd forgotten the reason for stalking after them. "Damn you. There's no way you could have heard me."

"He's so angry," Devlin said with a chuckle. "Who is this Eve he dreams of?"

"Her name is Evelyn Bromwell," Elliot said. "I asked around when I saw them dancing together."

Alexander could not control the rush of pure rage. He

flew at Elliot Markham and grabbed him by the throat. "Leave her the hell alone."

Elliot wrapped his hand around Alexander's and with equal strength pulled it away. "You have nothing to fear. I would never betray a brother by hurting someone he cared for."

"A brother?" Alexander spat. "You have mistaken me for someone else. So you can stop bloody well following me around and prying into my affairs. I won't tell you again."

The need to find Miss Bromwell and check that all was well overpowered all other thoughts and Alexander turned and strode towards the door. Besides, he had heard enough from these two degenerates.

"Better run home before sunrise," Devlin shouted. "Better not bite anyone on the way out."

Alexander froze. An icy chill seeped into his veins. They knew his secret. If he didn't silence them, his nightmare would soon become a reality.

He turned on his heels and marched back towards them.

Elliot held his hands up as a sign of surrender. "Wait. Show him, Leo. Show him why he's our brother."

Devlin stepped forward, shrugged out of his coat and waistcoat and threw them onto the bench. Yanking his shirt out of his breeches, he pulled it up to reveal the mark on his chest.

Alexander sucked in a breath. The mark: a cross inside a circle of thorny twine was identical to the one seared into his chest. It made no sense. That night in Bavaria, he had woken from the torturous dream to find his body branded with the unusual drawing. He'd not felt the iron burn his skin, nor did he know if the devil woman was responsible.

"I don't understand." Alexander shook his head. "We bear the same mark. But how did you come by it?"

"I have one, too," Elliot said, "ever since the night I met a golden-haired goddess with razor-sharp teeth. We call it the mark of the brotherhood."

"Well, the ladies seem to like it," Devlin added as he dressed.

Alexander struggled to comprehend what they were telling him. "The golden-haired woman said there were more, but I didn't think—"

"To find them in a ballroom in London," Elliot interjected.

A million and one questions flooded his mind. "Do you have the same ... the same afflictions?"

Devlin chuckled. "We live for the night. We have a desperate thirst for blood. We heard you call out to your lover."

Alexander gritted his teeth. "Miss Bromwell is not my lover."

"But you want her to be," Elliot said.

There was nothing he wanted more. But he could not risk hurting her. "How do you move about in society without ... without hurting anyone?"

They both looked at him as though he'd grown an extra head.

"Why would we hurt anyone?" Devlin said. "Oh, you mean biting people and draining their blood. As a mortal man, I loved beef. That doesn't mean I jumped on every cow I saw in a field. The occasional one, maybe."

"Ignore him. It is a case of control," Elliot said. "Anger doesn't help. When you're angry, you're more prone to unpredictability. Frustration is another trigger. That is why I readily accepted Lady Conley's offer. You'd be surprised what can be achieved with a calm mind. We have even trained our bodies to eat small amounts of food. It's not pleasant but ..."

"Do people not question why you do not move about in the day?"

"Most dissolute peers don't rise until three," Devlin said. "We are not any different. We are not the only men who fall into bed at dawn."

"How long have you been like this?" Alexander asked.

"Elliot is in his fourth year, me my third. If he had not come along when he did, I'd be dead. The loneliness was all-consuming. Like you, I was angry. I'd gotten into many a fight in the hope of being pierced through the heart."

"What about you?" Elliot asked.

"Two years." He had spent two long years believing he was alone, thinking no one would understand the beast that lurked inside. There'd been no one to talk to, no one to help him understand. His declaration raised another question. "Are there any others?"

Elliot shook his head. "Not that we know of. We only knew of you because we heard your call. When you heard our thoughts, you confirmed our suspicions."

"Come," Devlin said. "We're to attend a rather select party. You should come with us. Perhaps a night cradled between soft thighs will help calm your volatile spirit. The women we entertain have no desire for an emotional connection, and with your handsome face you'll prove popular."

Alexander shook his head as he was no longer the sort of man who enjoyed such vacuous pursuits. "I appreciate the offer, but I'll stay here."

"Miss Bromwell," Elliot whispered to Devlin, who raised his chin in acknowledgement. "Perhaps we could arrange a little party for him here. Something to soothe his troubled soul. Something he might find more appealing."

"You need not concern yourselves with me," Alexander replied.

Elliot reached into the pocket of his coat and removed a

card. "If you need anything, you'll find me here. Perhaps we may see you tomorrow night. Lady Westbury is having a ball in honour of her niece. When the young girls come out it always puts the other ladies in the mood for a bit of wild sport."

Alexander shrugged and placed Elliot's card in his pocket. He had no desire to parade around at another ball. He had come tonight for one reason only.

Wearing the same arrogant smirk, both gentlemen stepped forward and patted him on the back. "Until next time," they said in unison. "Welcome to the brotherhood."

CHAPTER 12

*C*harlotte Sutherby's rather quick recovery annoyed Evelyn. She could not shake the suspicion that it had all been an act to lure her away from Alexander. Indeed, as soon as the gentleman had disappeared, Charlotte felt considerably better. Usually, after swooning, one would feel nauseous or be plagued by a headache. Fresh air and a cup of hot tea were said to work wonders, but Charlotte insisted her brother fetch a double helping of ratafia.

Thoughts of being kissed by the enigmatic Alexander Cole refused to be tempered. Her mind conjured all sorts of scenarios involving a swim at midnight, a bench and a broken fountain. Whenever she reached the most exciting part of the daydream, Charlotte's whining sent the thoughts scattering like dead leaves in the wind.

"Miss Bromwell."

It took a tremendous effort not to shout "What!" and Evelyn turned to find a handsome gentleman with hair as dark as ebony and eyes a deep mesmerising green.

"Yes?" she said, the single word revealing her surprise.

Stupidly, she glanced left and right as though another lady had the same name and he had chosen the wrong one.

The gentleman bowed. "Forgive me. I know it is considered highly inappropriate as we have not been formally introduced, but I am Lord Markham. If I could just have a moment of your time." He paused and then added, "There is nothing to fear. We will remain in the ballroom, just a few feet away."

Evelyn turned to Charlotte, who looked down her nose and gave a disgruntled huff. Mr. Sutherby would return with refreshments at any moment. "Yes, of course, my lord," she said, relieved to have an excuse to leave the grumbling patient.

Lord Markham steered her away from Charlotte to a quieter spot near an alcove. "I could not help but notice you dancing with Lord Hale," he began. "I hope you do not think my approach forward or out of turn, but I recently saw the gentleman in the orangery and he appeared somewhat agitated."

"Agitated?" Evelyn repeated although it came as no surprise. No doubt he was annoyed with her for abandoning him without a word.

"It is probably nothing," he said with a dismissive wave. "I'm sure he will return momentarily. I did not mean to alarm you. It's just you appear to know him well. I suspect you will want to go to him." The gentleman stared into her eyes, and she found the rich green hues soothing. Images of rolling around in summer meadows and snoozing in the long grass filled her head. "I shall not keep you, as I'm sure you will want to find him."

Evelyn smiled. "Thank you, my lord, for bringing the matter to my attention."

"When you go to him, do not mention our conversation."

"No, my lord," she replied as the gentleman bowed and made his retreat.

You should go to him.

The thought popped into her head again. No one would notice her nipping out into the garden and she did owe Lord Hale an apology. Aunt Beatrice had spent the entire evening with Mr. Hartwood and would assume she was still with the Sutherbys.

With a quick glance over her shoulder, she slipped out into the night. She had no idea where she was going, but after a few wrong turns soon found herself outside the quaint little castle.

As soon as she opened the door and began her journey along the path, she knew Alexander Cole was still inside. Her body responded instantly. She felt the thrum of excitement tingle in her fingertips, working its way up her arm to fill her chest.

She found him sitting on a stone bench, his head in his hands, evoking memories of him at Stony Cross, of how glorious his naked body looked in the moonlight.

"Lord Hale?"

He looked up at her. His eyes were filled with sorrow, and her heart swelled so large she could feel it pushing against her ribs. The overwhelming urge to soothe him, to run her fingers through his dark locks, took hold.

"Miss Bromwell," he said, coming to his feet. He glanced towards the door. "What are you doing in here?"

"I left you without any explanation. It was rude of me. Miss Sutherby had fainted and well ..."

"I am normally the one guilty of being rude. But you should not be seen with me. Not out here."

Desire pulsed deep in her core at the thought of being alone with him. She could not stop her gaze lingering on his mouth as she recalled his comment about wanting to kiss her.

"I do not care about that." She stepped closer. "No one

knows I am out here." A strange energy pulsed around them, and she wanted to throw her arms wide and embrace it.

He closed the gap between them. "Come, let us return to the ballroom before someone sees you."

She didn't want to go back. She might never get another opportunity to be alone with him, to explore this potent attraction that existed between them.

"What you said earlier … about what you would want if we were alone."

"They were the foolish words of a dreamer."

"You did not mean it then?"

The corners of his mouth twitched. "Oh, I meant every word."

"Then kiss me," she whispered, aware of the tremor in her voice, of the brazen way she had asked. She raised a trembling hand to his cheek, and his eyes grew wide. His skin felt cool to the touch, soft where he'd recently shaved. He covered her hand with his own, securing it in place as he closed his eyes.

Taking advantage of the moment, she stood on the tips of her toes and pressed her lips to his. From the briefest touch, the world erupted around her, the spark of recognition, of familiarity flowing from his lips.

He was her match in every way.

She felt it to be true; she knew it to be true.

He opened his eyes, the blue rays penetrating her soul and she thought her legs would buckle beneath her.

"You don't know what you're doing to me," he gasped when she pulled away. "You don't know what I would give to kiss you as I want to."

"Do it," she replied, failing to hide her desperation. With him, all inhibitions were lost.

"I do not want to hurt you."

"I trust you. We will never know what exists between us unless you try. We will never understand it."

She thought he would protest, but his arm slid around her back, pulled her to his hard body as his mouth claimed hers.

The fire in her belly ignited in a blaze of desperate longing. Even with her lack of experience, she could not control the urge to taste him, to deepen the kiss and yet she sensed he was holding back.

"I need more," she said, breaking contact.

His mouth curved into the beginnings of a smile, and she wanted to cry. The glorious sight affected her like nothing else before.

"You want what I cannot give you," he said, his smile fading.

She refused to accept his answer. Stripping off her gloves and throwing them to the floor, she pushed her hands up over his chest and threaded them around his neck. "Kiss me again, Alexander. Like you want to. Like you mean it."

A growl emanated from the back of his throat and he claimed her mouth fiercely. There was no slow coaxing. His tongue penetrated the line of her lips and thrust deeply, wildly into her mouth.

She clutched at his shoulders, needing to be near him as she found the courage to meet him with the same uncontrollable level of intensity. Desire roared in her ears when her tongue danced with his, and his hands drifted down her back to draw her closer so she could feel the hard evidence of his arousal.

Nothing had ever felt so wonderful.

Nothing had ever felt so perfect.

"Oh, God, Eve," he whispered, raining urgent kisses along the line of her jaw. "I wish we were naked, swimming in the river at night."

Feeling a throbbing sensation between her legs, she

grabbed the lapels of his coat. "I don't understand this. I don't understand what is happening to me, but I don't care."

He claimed her mouth again, delving inside, pressing his body into her again and again, the rhythmical motion making her dizzy with desire. His ragged breathing and deep groans made her feel so drunk she hardly noticed his hand creeping up under her gown, not until his fingers brushed her most intimate place.

"Alexander," she panted. The need to feel close to him banished any shame or fear.

"I can't stop," he whispered hoarsely. "I can't stop touching you."

"I want you to touch me," she said softly. The ropes of restraint no longer existed between them.

As she floated away on a cloud of ecstasy, he stroked her back and forth, his tongue thrusting into her mouth simultaneously. Her whole body edged closer to some unknown destination, a place far beyond this world. Pleasure rippled through her as she rubbed against his hand, consumed by this madness for him.

He quickened the pace.

The room burst forth in a blaze of glittering lights. She felt her body convulse at his touch, and she pushed her tongue into his mouth, searching for something more, desperate to prolong the feeling.

In a distant recess of her mind, she heard the rustle of material as he removed his hand, and she felt the loss like a deep ache in her heart.

He drew her to his chest as the tremors subsided. "I have never felt anything as powerful as this," he panted against her hair. "It has taken all the strength I have not to spread you wide and push inside you."

She sucked in a breath at his honesty. "I have never known a feeling like this, either. All I know is that I could never marry Mr. Sutherby," she said. How could she when her soul sang only for this man? Whatever happened, she could never give herself to another.

Alexander sighed. She could sense his pain as he held her tighter. "I cannot marry. I would not make a good husband."

Evelyn pulled away and looked up at him. "I think you would make a fine husband."

An image of them at Stony Cross surrounded by a horde of children flashed into her mind.

"I do not want children," he replied as though reading her thoughts.

There was a shift in him, a wave of coldness that acted as a shroud to hide any emotion. He had been living the life of a recluse. Perhaps these strange feelings were new to him, made him overcautious, wary.

"I am not asking for a declaration," she said. "You do not have to convince me of your unsuitability."

He stroked the outline of her face. "What are you asking?"

"I am not asking for anything."

It was a lie.

She wanted everything.

"After what has just happened, you should be demanding I make you an offer."

"I would never want what you were not willing to give. You wanted to touch me, and I wanted it, too. No one else need know of it and so let that be the end of the matter."

Evelyn thought her response would calm him. She expected him to express relief, but she knew anger simmered beneath the surface.

"What if I don't want it to be the end of the matter?" he said. "What would you say if I kissed you again?"

"I think you know the answer."

He turned away from her, thrust his hands through his

hair and sighed loudly at the glass ceiling before swinging back round to face her. "So you have decided to refuse Mr. Sutherby?"

Evelyn narrowed her gaze. "I cannot believe you need to ask after what has just occurred."

"But what of your financial stability?"

She shrugged. "What of it? As you rightly said, it should not be a factor in my decision. Love is the only consideration, and I do not love Mr. Sutherby."

But I am falling in love with you, she added silently.

The thought caused her throat to constrict as a rush of conflicting emotions took hold. Excitement sprouted like blossom on a tree: something bright and new and pretty. Desire unfurled in her belly. A feeling of rapturous joy filled her heart. But they all existed beneath a cloud of uncertainty and fear.

Tears threatened to fall as though she was already grieving for the loss and she knew she must leave. If he kissed her again, she would not be able to suppress the need to devour him, to lie naked beneath him, to let him take whatever he wanted from her.

"I should get back before I am missed." She turned away and took a deep breath. "I will be at Lady Westbury's ball tomorrow evening if you wish to talk."

If he came to the ball, then there was a chance he felt something, too. If he returned to Stony Cross, she knew she would never see him again.

She strode away from him, the first few steps the hardest to take.

"Eve," he called out to her, his tone softer than she had ever heard it before. "I can't be the man you want me to be."

Her stomach twisted into painful knots. "We shall see," she said, glancing over her shoulder and forcing a smile.

All she could do was hope and pray he was wrong.

CHAPTER 13

"You must excuse my brother," Charlotte Sutherby said, patting Evelyn's arm. "I begged him not to cancel your stroll in the park, but when I swooned at the foot of the stairs, he refused to leave me alone."

"I understand," Evelyn said, trying to glance about Lady Westbury's ballroom without her companions noticing. In truth, she'd been relieved to read Mr. Sutherby's note. It had given her a little more time to prepare for the awkward conversation, should he decide to propose. "It gave me an opportunity to spend the afternoon with my aunt."

Aunt Beatrice had failed to make an appearance at breakfast. Mr. Hartwood, having escorted them home from Lord Melbury's ball, had stayed until the early hours, drinking and playing cards.

"Perhaps I can make amends this evening, Miss Bromwell. The night is warm and clear. A stroll around the gardens would be a welcome diversion."

Evelyn hesitated. If she missed Alexander's arrival, she might never find him in the crush. But then she had spent the last two hours watching the door, her heart skipping a beat whenever a new face appeared. She had to accept the possibility that he'd returned to his dilapidated hideaway in the New Forest—his heart, as well as the rusty gates, barred to all intruders.

"Charlotte will stroll with us, just a few steps ahead," Mr. Sutherby added with a dandified wave. "And I do need to stretch my legs after being cooped up indoors all day."

"You are such a considerate brother, Nicholas." Charlotte beamed. She turned to Evelyn. "I know of no other gentleman so devoted to his family."

Nor a sister so devoted, Evelyn thought. Charlotte Sutherby's beauty radiated from her like a beacon. Yet she'd shown no interest in any other gentlemen. Securing her brother's happiness appeared to be Charlotte's only motivation.

"I shall just go and inform my aunt," Evelyn said, deciding she would accompany them. It was only right that she should explain her feelings to Mr. Sutherby. He deserved the truth, and she knew of other young ladies who would be only too pleased to be seen on the arm of such a dashing gentleman. "Wait for me near the terrace."

With one last glance at the empty doorway, Evelyn traipsed about the ballroom in search of her aunt. She spotted her dancing with Mr. Hartwood, exchanged a reassuring smile and made her way to the terrace.

Failing to notice Evelyn's approach, Charlotte Sutherby's countenance had changed dramatically. The innocent smile had been abandoned, only to be replaced with the wild look of the Devil. With clenched teeth and a furrowed brow, she grabbed the sleeve of her brother's coat and grumbled in his ear. Like a naughty child, Mr. Sutherby cast his gaze to the floor and nodded. When her gaze locked with Evelyn's, her hand grew limp and fell to her side, the irate expression turning soft and serene.

"Ah, Miss Bromwell," she said, her tone light and airy. "I

… I was just complaining to Nicholas, how lax of him not to escort you to your aunt."

Mr. Sutherby made no comment and forced a smile as he offered his arm. Evelyn placed a hesitant hand in the crook, her fingers barely touching the material.

They followed Charlotte down the steps and out across the illuminated lawn. Evelyn could feel Mr. Sutherby's assessing gaze, and she shivered as though frozen fingers trailed along the neckline of her gown.

"Is there something you wish to discuss?" Evelyn asked, desperate to bring an end to the matter. Of course, she would need to explain her decision to her aunt, who had already expressed her approval of the match.

"You know me so well, Miss Bromwell, I believe you can read my thoughts. It's such a comfort when one finds the person who is their match, their intellectual equal. A person who can make life's journey all the more pleasurable."

"I do not believe intelligence should be the deciding factor when it comes to matrimony, Mr. Sutherby. We must follow our heart, not our mind. It is the only way to be true to ourselves." She pictured Alexander Cole's handsome face, knowing her soul sang only to his tune.

Mr. Sutherby gave a contemptuous snort. "The heart is a fickle thing, Miss Bromwell. It leaves us prone to indulge in fanciful notions, to dream of a grand passion and a blissful union."

Evelyn had felt such a passion and would gladly indulge her heart if only given a chance. "I want all of those things. I am sorry to disappoint you, Mr. Sutherby, but I could not settle for anything less. If I must dream until I am in my dotage, then so be it."

She felt the gentleman stiffen. There should be no need for him to offer for her now, not when she had made her position perfectly clear.

As they approached a tall topiary hedge, Charlotte stopped to wait for them. "I hear Lady Westbury has spent a small fortune on an outdoor aviary. Indeed, I believe I can hear the birds chirping. Perhaps it is through here."

With some reluctance, Evelyn allowed Mr. Sutherby to escort her through the narrow walkway believing the sooner they pandered to Charlotte's whims the quicker they could return to the ballroom.

"I'm convinced it is down here," Charlotte said, running along the gravel path before disappearing around the corner.

When they reached the bottom of the path, Charlotte was nowhere in sight.

"Where on earth has she got to?" Evelyn said. It was not wise for a lady to be lost in the dark on her own.

"Do not worry about Charlotte," Mr. Sutherby said. "She can't be far away. She'll find her way back to us."

An uncomfortable sense of foreboding settled in Evelyn's chest. "Perhaps we should head back the way we came," she said, moving to walk in front.

But Mr. Sutherby grabbed her by her wrist and swung her back around to face him. "Let's try this way," he said, pulling her further along the path.

Evelyn tried to yank her arm free, but the gentleman was much stronger than she expected. "Mr. Sutherby. Will you please let go of my arm?"

"Do not play the coy, little miss. You have been teasing me from the moment we entered the garden, with your dreams of a passionate union." He stopped and pulled her to his chest. "Why wait until your dotage? I am more than happy to indulge you now."

Alexander sauntered into the ballroom, aware of the whispers and odd glances as those who were absent from Lord Melbury's soiree were informed of the latest gossip.

He had decided not to attend. The workings of his rational mind knew there was no hope of a union with Evelyn Bromwell. No lady would choose to live with a monster. A lady wanted marriage, children and picnics in the park under the midday sun. She did not want to roam about in the darkness like an empty soul lost to the night. The curse thrust upon him would plague him for all eternity. He would never be free to indulge in his passion.

Yet still he'd come.

He could not deny the burning in his chest when she entered his thoughts. He could not stop his body responding to the mere sound of her voice. The raging passion that writhed inside him could not be tempered. For his own sanity, he had no choice but to follow his heart.

What did he have to lose?

"Hale. Over here."

Alexander glanced around the outskirts of the packed ballroom. Elliot Markham was propped up against the wall, his arms folded across his chest as he raised his chin to beckon Alexander over.

"On your own tonight?" Alexander asked. "Or is Devlin busy taking advantage of a married lady's generosity?"

"No. The idiot is dancing." With his mouth forming a scowl, Elliot nodded to the dance floor. "Look at him, prancing about like the fool of the fair. Next, he'll be waving bright ribbons and handing out trinkets."

The corners of Alexander's mouth twitched in amusement. "Why should that be a problem?"

"He is dancing with Cassandra Reed." Elliot sighed. "Lady Westbury's virgin niece. As soon as he saw her, his eyes swelled to the size of billiard balls. I'm surprised they're not mopping up the floor from his excessive salivating."

"I have some sympathy. Drooling is something I am learning to live with."

Elliot straightened. "Ah, you refer to the delightful Miss Bromwell. Am I the only brother who feels nauseous at the thought of bedding a virgin?"

"Judging by the lecherous smile on Devlin's face, I'd say yes."

Elliot stepped closer and whispered, "I swear, if he drinks from her I'll rip his throat right out."

Alexander jerked his head, surprised at Elliot's volatile reaction, although it felt good to talk so openly about something he'd considered so despicable. It almost made him feel human.

"You believe he would?"

"It would not be the first time I have been left to clean up his mess."

Alexander inhaled sharply. "Devlin's killed someone?"

"No," Elliot replied, shaking his head. "Of course not. But let's just say he likes the taste of virgin blood. He said it tastes clean, untainted, like drinking water from a mountain stream as opposed to the sludge found in the Thames. I think it's all in his head. He has convinced himself it's the blood, but I believe he still dreams of his youth, of frolicking with debutantes in the hope of finding true love."

Alexander's thoughts flashed to Miss Bromwell, and he scoured the sea of heads in the hope of spotting her. Strangely, he had no desire to drink from her. What he felt for her went beyond the need for personal gratification.

"Your Miss Bromwell is taking a turn about the garden with her companions," Elliot said with a smirk. "I assume that's who you're looking for."

Alexander glanced at the terrace doors. "Is it so obvious?"

Elliot patted him on the back. "You forget I can feel the

passion emanating from you. You feel deeply for her. That much is obvious."

"Regardless of my feelings, the situation is hopeless," Alexander replied with a frustrated sigh.

"Which is why I chose an uncomplicated life, a life without any emotional attachment. It is unrealistic to hope that any woman would accept us for what we are."

While he acknowledged the logic in Elliot's words, his heart fought desperately against the possibility that Evelyn would turn away from him if she knew. "I used to believe that. To an extent, I still do. But I've come here tonight in the hope I'm wrong."

"Then I wish you luck, my friend, as you're going to need a barrow full of it." Elliot nodded beyond Alexander's shoulder. "Here comes your lady now."

Alexander turned to see Charlotte Sutherby hurry through the terrace doors into the ballroom. He held his breath while he waited for a glimpse of Evelyn's wide eyes and pretty pout, his heart beating erratically as excitement thrummed through his veins.

But Miss Sutherby was alone.

"You're sure Miss Bromwell went out walking with that lady?" Alexander said, tapping Elliot on the arm to focus his attention.

Elliot narrowed his gaze. "Yes. She went out with her and a fair-haired gentleman. They've probably just fallen behind."

Alexander stood in frozen silence, each passing second feeling more like an hour. "I'm going out to find her."

"Ah, you fear she's interested in the other gentleman," Elliot said with a chuckle.

"It is not a laughing matter. I do not trust Mr. Sutherby. There's something shifty about him. He intends to make Miss Bromwell an offer of marriage. What if he refused to take no for an answer?"

"What if she said yes and you stumble upon a lovers' tryst?"

Anger sprang forth, roused from its dark, dank lair. "Damn you," Alexander whispered through gritted teeth, resisting the urge to throttle someone, anyone. "Miss Bromwell will not accept him. Something is wrong. I sense it."

Without another word, he turned on his heels and marched away, pushing through the crowd until he reached the terrace. One quick scan of the empty lawn confirmed his fear. Miss Bromwell must be in a secluded area of the garden.

Had she gone of her own volition?

Or did Sutherby have more sinister intentions in mind?

CHAPTER 14

*A*lexander charged out into the night, his mind too chaotic to pick up any lingering trace of Evelyn's emotional imprint.

"Damnation," Elliot shouted, skidding across the grass behind him. "Wait for me."

"I don't need you to come."

"You're in the mind for murder," Elliot said, keeping up with Alexander's long strides. "Someone needs to be in control if we are to protect the secret of the brotherhood."

"I don't give a damn about the bloody brotherhood. If Sutherby hurts her in any—"

Alexander.

The word wrenched at his heart.

The silent plea forced him to come to an abrupt halt and survey his surroundings. There was no sign of anyone in the garden, but he felt a tug deep in his core drawing him to the tall hedge. The dark pathway beyond beckoned him to enter.

Elliot stopped at his side. "I heard it, too. It came from inside that topiary tunnel."

As soon as Alexander crossed the entrance, fear

enveloped him like a curtain of cobwebs, clinging to his chest and shoulders, his body jerking back in response.

"They're definitely in here," Elliot said, "I can hear voices, someone struggling."

Alexander gulped a breath as he raced along the narrow walkway. The path branched both left and right. Instinctively, he felt compelled to take the route to the left.

"Get the hell off me! What's wrong with you?"

Evelyn's desperate curse ignited the anger simmering in his gut.

"Come now. You've been playing games with me for weeks," Sutherby said.

Elliot gripped Alexander's shoulder. "Don't do anything foolish," he whispered as they spotted Sutherby pinning Evelyn against the hedge.

"Get your bloody hands off her," Alexander roared, tearing along the path.

As though chastising a disobedient pup, he grabbed Sutherby by the collar of his coat, thrust him high in the air before throwing him to the ground. With legs and arms flailing, Sutherby covered his head with his hands as Alexander yanked him back to his feet.

"Wait. Don't hit me. It's not what it seems. We are betrothed."

Alexander froze, his clenched fist suspended in mid-air as his chest grew empty and hollow.

"We are not betrothed," Evelyn said, rushing to his side. "I have made it clear I do not want to marry him, but he will not accept it."

"But your aunt has already approved the match," Sutherby countered. "She said you were in agreement."

"Then she misled you."

"But you said you had dreams of a grand passion and a blissful union."

"I was not talking about you."

Elliot gave a discreet cough.

"You mean you're talking about him?" Sutherby's gaze shot to Alexander, his twisted face showing his disdain. "Why, I should call the gentleman out for stealing another man's betrothed."

Evelyn gave an exasperated sigh. "How many times must I tell you? We are not betrothed, Mr. Sutherby."

"Call me out?" Alexander echoed gripping Sutherby by the lapels of his coat. "I could just save myself the bother." His teeth began to ache, and he flexed his jaw. The dull throbbing would escalate until he'd pierced skin and drawn blood. "I could just throttle you here and now."

Elliot muttered a curse. "It is just a simple misunderstanding," he said, his tone revealing an element of panic. He placed his hand on Alexander's arm, the grip firm, unyielding. "Let me escort Mr. Sutherby back to the ballroom. He'll not trouble anyone again. I'm sure Miss Bromwell does not wish to see such a violent display."

Alexander glanced to his right; Evelyn's eyes were wide, a little fearful.

"If you want to live to see dawn," Alexander said, releasing Sutherby, "I suggest you go with Lord Markham."

"Then I am taking Miss Bromwell with me," Sutherby blurted as he craned his neck and straightened his coat.

A growl resonated from the back of Alexander's throat. "Miss Bromwell is staying with me."

"I don't th-think that's for you to decide," Sutherby stuttered.

Elliot stepped in front of Alexander and took Mr. Sutherby's arm. "I think you want to come with me. I think you want to return to the ballroom. We will return now."

Mr. Sutherby's eyes glazed over and without another word he complied with Markham's request. As he stepped past Alexander, he said, "I think I should return to the ball-room, but it is not the end of the matter. I will not relinquish my claim so easily."

"Your claim?" Evelyn cried. "I am no man's property, sir, and you'll do well to remember it."

Alexander could feel his anger rising again.

"Not here," Elliot whispered, leaning closer. "Not now. I fear the gentleman may make a scene to force the lady's hand. You must see Miss Bromwell home, and I will speak to her aunt. I'm convinced she'll be happy to know you were here to intervene. Call on me later. There is something we need to discuss." He nodded his head to indicate he was refer-ring to Mr. Sutherby.

"Very well. I shall call as soon as I've seen Miss Bromwell safely to her door."

Alexander watched them walk away, aware that Evelyn hovered at his shoulder.

They were alone once again. His body responded instantly. In his mind, he imagined pushing her up against the hedge, devouring her mouth, thrusting inside her sweet core as she wrapped her legs around him. The need to have her felt like a loud drum beating through his veins, the tempo increasing with every breath.

"I called you, and you came," she said, placing her hand on his arm. "How did you know where to find me?"

He could not turn to face her. He refused to behave like a scoundrel and force himself on her as Sutherby had done.

"Lord Markham noticed you'd not returned to the ball-room. It was the only logical place to look," he said, covering her hand and moving it to the crook of his arm. "Let me escort you home."

"Are you angry with me?"

"No."

"Tell me you don't believe what Mr. Sutherby said. It's

utter nonsense. I have never agreed to a betrothal. I would never have kissed you had there been a prior arrangement."

"I know."

Why did she have to mention kissing? He was struggling to partake in even the simplest conversation.

They strode across the grass and out through the gate leading to the mews.

"It is best we don't go back to get your cape. Will you be warm enough if we walk?"

"What in these slippers? Can we not simply hail a hackney?"

He glanced down at her feet and shook his head. "I never ride in a closed carriage. I never ride in any form of carriage. Where do you live?"

"Duke Street. But we can access the garden from Great Ryder Street. It will be more discreet. I can show you the way. It's not far."

"I know the way, but I'll take a detour along the quieter streets. Would you like my coat?"

"No, thank you. I'm perfectly fine. It's quite warm tonight."

They walked along in silence, the air about them still buzzing with restrained desire. It felt uncomfortable. The muscles in his shoulders were stiff, tense. His heartbeat was so erratic he could feel it pumping in his throat.

"We must hurry," he said, quickening his pace, the need to protect her his only concern.

"Why don't you ride in a carriage?" she asked, sounding a little breathless. Her fingers flexed over the muscle in his arm, sending a pulse of energy shooting down to his groin. "I assume an earl would have more than one."

The question threw him off kilter. What the hell was he supposed to say? Stepping into the carriage in Bavaria was akin to stepping through the gateway to Hell.

"I experienced a rather horrendous event in a carriage. I prefer to avoid them for fear of being hounded by the memory."

Her fingers dug into his arm. "Was it the accident you had a few years ago? Is it why people assumed you were disfigured?"

Fragments of distorted images flashed into his mind. "Do you mind if we talk about something else?"

He could feel her gaze searching his face, drifting down over his chest. "Why did you come to the ball tonight?"

Damnation. Why did she persist in asking awkward questions?

"You forgot your gloves. You threw them on the floor in the orangery, and I thought you might be in need of them."

She laughed, the sound soft and enchanting. "Why must you always skirt around the truth? Are you afraid to be honest with me?"

He turned to meet her gaze, his stomach lurching at the sight of her bright eyes and warm smile. "What do you want me to say? Do you want me to tell you that all I can think about is kissing you? That I dream of covering your body with mine? That just being near you heals my damaged soul?"

"Yes," she said softly. "Tell me what is in your heart, Alexander. I want to know everything."

Everything? How could he tell her his darkest secret, his worst nightmare? She would never look at him in the same way again. Those pretty blue eyes would lose their lustrous quality, a black cloud of fear and loathing obscuring their brilliance.

"Is it not enough to know that I want you?"

"It is enough for now."

Her words sent a frisson of fear through him which he tried to dismiss.

They turned into the mews off Great Ryder, the privacy giving him the opportunity to pull her arm tighter through his.

"It is this door," she said, pointing to the wooden gate in the middle of a long brick wall.

He walked her to the entrance. "Will a servant be waiting to let you in?"

"If not, I can always break a window." She came to stand in front of him. Her eyes stared longingly into his, asking him to kiss her, begging him to.

"That reminds me, you still need to pay for the damage to my window."

"Pay?" she said with a giggle. "What choice did I have? You refused to let me in."

I can't let you in now, he thought. *Not if it means facing rejection.* He brought her fingers to his mouth and brushed his lips across them. "I shall wait here until you've closed the door, until I know you're safely inside. Goodnight, Miss Bromwell."

She swallowed deeply, and her bottom lip quivered. "Will … will I see you again?"

"I don't know."

"What are you scared of?"

"Only of hurting you," he said before stepping past her and opening the gate. He already knew how to live with disappointment and pain. "Please, go inside. You must go inside."

She moved through the doorway and turned to face him, hugging the edge of the gate as though it brought comfort.

"You must close the door." He knew she had no choice but to obey.

When he heard the latch click, he took a deep breath. His body shook with need, his heart ached, his cock throbbed. He could still sense her standing on the other side of the door.

Yet the tumultuous nature of her emotions made it more difficult to access her mood.

Heart-wrenching pain hit him first, with such force that he sucked in a breath. He could feel the pulse of desire, too, mingled with a soul-deep yearning that cried out to him.

Bloody hell.

He had to walk away. He had to leave her. But his feet were rooted firmly to the ground. Letting his head fall back, he stared up into the darkness. But he knew he would not find the strength or the courage he needed there.

I love you, Alexander.

The words exploded in his chest like the brightest firework, bursting through him in a mass of warm, wondrous rays.

He had begun the night wanting to believe there was hope, yet he'd closed the door to it at every opportunity. Convinced himself it was all in vain. Acceptance was all he wanted. And love … to love and feel loved in return.

With a burst of optimism, he turned on his heels and moved towards the door.

He would tell her about his past; he would tell her everything.

CHAPTER 15

*H*er heart was breaking. She had known Alexander Cole for a short time, barely knew the man he kept hidden inside. Yet she loved him with every ounce of her being.

How was it possible?

From the moment she closed the gate, the feeling of loss was unbearable. Tears formed. Perhaps she had lived many lives with him before, each new birth erasing her memory of the last. Somewhere, the essence of the man must still be buried deep in her consciousness, reminding her that she had always known him, always loved him.

He felt it, too; she was sure of it.

So why was he so hesitant? What was he afraid of?

The sound of wood scraping against gravel startled her, and she swung around to find his muscular shoulders filling the doorway. Her heart lurched at the sight, fluttering in her chest like a bird trying to escape its cage, as he closed the door and stepped forward.

"I know I shouldn't be here, but I can't leave you." The tremor in his voice suggested an inner turmoil. "I am too weak to deny my heart and soul what it so desperately desires."

She could hear her own breathless pants as he came to stand with her beneath the cherry tree.

"I want to tell you everything," he continued, using his thumb to wipe the tear from her cheek. "Afterwards, you may insist I leave, but it is a chance I must take."

Evelyn didn't care what he had to tell her. It was all in the past. Nothing he could say would change the way she felt about him. Nothing could dampen her desire, or extinguish the love burning in her heart.

He took her chin between his thumb and forefinger. "Don't be afraid. You need never be afraid of me. You must know I would never hurt you."

A surge of raw emotion burst forth. She wanted to ease his torment, make him forget all the terrible things that plagued him, make him smile and laugh. Whatever he had to say could wait.

Love was unconditional; she would prove it to him.

No matter what happened, she was his. Now. Tonight. Forever.

God had granted them this precious moment, and she would grab it with both hands and never let it go.

Before he could utter another word, she tried to thread her arms around his neck, but he caught her hands and held them tight.

"I shall give you this opportunity to step away, to go inside and leave me here alone. For I promise you, when our lips meet, I cannot control what happens between us."

Evelyn swallowed deeply as she understood the implication of his words. "I would never run away from you."

"If you value your virtue, you will turn from me and not look back."

"I want to stay." Her heart was racing. "I want everything

you have to give, Alexander. I want to be with you, regardless of the consequences."

He gave her no option to reconsider. As the last word left her lips, he lowered his head and claimed her mouth in a surge of unbridled passion.

The kiss was wild, chaotic. Their frantic hands grasped and tugged at each other's clothing. Their tongues danced amidst pants and guttural groans. Evelyn threaded her hands into his hair and pulled at the roots to anchor his mouth to hers.

His masculine scent surrounded her, potent and intoxicating. The urge to touch him, to feel the heat radiate from his skin became unbearable, and she pulled her mouth away from his.

Swallowing a series of short breaths she fumbled with his coat, pushing it over his broad shoulders, abandoning it to yank at the buttons on his waistcoat.

"We should slow down," he panted, "but I can't stop."

"Quick. I need to be near you." Her voice sounded different—deeper, huskier. Desperate.

At her command, he shrugged his arms out of the sleeves of his coat, and it fell to the ground.

He kissed her again, hard and swift, before turning her around to fiddle with the buttons on her dress.

"Bloody hell, I can't see what I'm doing. My fingers feel numb."

"Quick," she repeated. "Just rip it."

He turned her around to face him as his lips curved up into a wicked grin. "Rip it?" he asked, his eyes alight with amusement.

The beauty of it was enough to send her spiralling further into the madness that consumed her and she yanked at the bodice until she heard the material tear. He helped her out of her gown, grasping her petticoat as the silk pooled around her feet. The hooks and eyelets gave way easily under the strain as he ripped them apart. It took him less than a minute to untie her short stays.

Once free from her encumbrance, his hands moved everywhere, all at once. He caressed her breasts through the thin chemise, cupping her and pulling her against the evidence of his arousal, kissed and nuzzled her neck.

Then he stopped suddenly, pulled away and stared at the column of her throat with some confusion.

"What's wrong?"

He shook his head and with another grin said, "Nothing. I was worried I might hurt you, but it seems my fears were unfounded."

"By kissing my neck?"

"I have sharp teeth."

"I found it rather pleasant." She sensed a slight reservation and decided to offer an incentive to rouse his passion again. "I am yours, Alexander." She pulled her chemise up over her head until she stood naked before him. "I promise you there will never be another."

"Eve." The word held a hint of anguish.

Heat pulsed between her legs, craving his touch. With her gaze never leaving his, she crouched and lay down amidst the mounds of material. "Take me, Alexander." Her words were brazen and wicked and sinful; but she didn't care. "I'm yours. Only yours."

Like a man possessed, he tore at his clothes until he was naked.

She had never seen such a glorious sight.

When he pressed his body on top of hers, she thought she would melt from the fire coursing through her.

He claimed her lips as he rubbed against her, his tongue dancing with hers, their mouths mating.

"I will never let you go," he said as he moved to lavish her breasts with equal attention.

It was all too much—exquisite pleasure mingled with an agonising longing. She needed something more from him, something she could not explain in words.

"Alexander, please."

"Oh, God, Eve. I will die if I don't have you soon."

He moved back up to claim her mouth, used his knee to push her legs apart. She felt him nudge against the intimate place where the fire burned and pulsed.

"I'll be careful. I'll … holy hell," he gasped as he pushed inside her.

"Oh," she breathed. Swallowing hard, she clutched at the muscles in his back, wrapped her legs around him as he edged deeper.

It felt heavenly, divine. She felt whole, complete.

Then he was kissing her again, his tongue in her mouth, moving down to her breasts as he thrust past her virginity. She cried out, the sound drifting up into the night and he stilled as she grew accustomed to the feel of him.

The rush of pure emotion made her want to cry. She wanted to show him how much she cared for him, how much this moment meant to her.

"I love you," she whispered as he moved back and forth inside her, knowing that in doing so she exposed her soul, had laid it bare.

"You're mine." He growled as he pounded deeper and deeper, the rhythmical slapping teasing her senses. "Forever. Always."

She moved with him, let him control the pace, let him claim what he needed as she relished in the feel of the bulging muscles in his arms. The need to claim him in return, to have him at her mercy, burned inside her.

"Show me," she said between breathless pants. "Show me how to make you mine. Show me how to claim you."

⁓

Alexander stilled. The feel of her sweet body hugging his cock made him reluctant to withdraw, but he could not deny both his surprise and fascination at her request.

He glanced over his shoulder. "We'll need to move," he said, almost groaning aloud when he slid out of her warmth and moved back to lean against the trunk of the cherry tree.

Her eyes grew wide as her gaze fell to his jutting length. "Sit astride me," he commanded, and she crawled over to him and straddled his thighs. It took all his effort not to take the rosy peak of her deliciously round breast into his mouth, but he concentrated on positioning himself at her entrance. "Sit on me. Lower yourself down but do it slowly."

Gripping his shoulders with both hands, Evelyn did as he asked, impaling herself as she took the length of him deep inside.

"Oh, God." He threw his head back against the trunk. "Take me, Eve. Take me as your own." He gripped her hips and directed her movements until she found a rhythm.

Without the comfort of a mattress, it made it difficult for him to thrust up into her and he was left to rely on her to stimulate him.

With his hands cupping her buttocks, he watched the enchanting display. The night was clear; the moon's muted rays brushed her skin. Her hair had come loose and hung wildly about her shoulders. Her lips were swollen and parted as her breathing became ragged. The moist sound that accompanied their joining was the sweetest song he'd ever heard. Nothing else in his life had ever matched the magnificence of this moment.

"Lean over me a little," he said, and he took her nipple in his mouth, used his fingers to rub against her as she slid up and down his length.

He struggled to hold back as her hips moved more erratically. The coil of desire wound tighter and tighter and he knew it would not be long before she found her release.

Amidst the soft moans, she whispered his name, bucked and writhed, and he grabbed her hips and rocked her back and forth, desperate to maintain the rhythm.

"Say you are mine," he said, his voice a deep growl as her inner muscles hugged and pumped his cock.

"I … I'm yours, Alexander," she cried as they found their release together.

CHAPTER 16

*W*ith his arms wrapped around her, Alexander held Eve against his body and waited while their breathing slowed to a regular rate. He was still buried inside her although his ability to perform had diminished.

Until a few days ago, the thought of spending time in the company of another person roused feelings of anger, of betrayal. The belief that he was unable to control the violent urges, coupled with the lucid nightmares of him draining the life from all those who crossed his path, left him living in a permanent shadow of fear.

He had prayed many times: to be transported back to the tavern, to be free of the agony, to ease his loneliness. Little did he know, Evelyn Bromwell would storm into his life to answer his prayers.

Eve stirred and lifted her head from his shoulder, damp tendrils of hair obscuring her face. Never, amongst the vast array of licentious encounters, had he ever felt so sated.

"Are you all right?" he asked, smoothing back the tangled locks. Her eyes held a look he'd seen many times before—

heavy lids framing a dreamy gaze. But on her, the magnificence caused his body to flame.

"I'm fine." She bent her head and kissed him once, her lips slightly parted. "I would happily do it all over again."

"I might need a few minutes, but I am more than willing."

She tapped him lightly on the chest. "I meant I don't regret giving myself to you."

No one had ever given him such a precious gift. "Was it what you imagined it would be?" He caressed her back as he spoke, the contact making him swell inside her.

Her eyes widened at the sensation, and she swallowed deeply before replying. "I didn't know I would feel like that. It was as though my soul floated out of my body. Everything went hazy, and a tingling sensation rippled through me."

No one had ever spoken to him so openly, so honestly, and he felt privileged to have been the one to rouse such a satisfying response.

"We should have found a more suitable place," he said, a stab of guilt piercing his chest. "Somewhere warm, a little more comfortable."

"But I like it out here." She looked up at the night sky. The stars twinkled against the vast, inky background. The celestial canopy was a fitting setting for such a heavenly experience. "We have an affinity for the night, for indulging our whims in secret. It is what first attracted me to you. It is only right we indulge our desires in the same manner."

God had not forsaken him. God had sent this angel of light to be his salvation, to be his companion, to walk with him in the shadows.

"I feel free at night," he said, his tone a little melancholic. "The night is my home. It is where I belong."

Ironically, the night was also his prison.

"Sometimes the darkness calls out to me." She stared at a point beyond him. "It rouses me from sleep, forcing me to lie awake until dawn. I have always found it a lonely time, as though I have woken to find I am the only person alive in the world."

Alexander stroked her face. His fingers trailed down her neck, over a pert pink nipple, and he smiled when she sucked in a breath.

"You don't have to be alone at night. Know that I am always awake, always waiting for you."

Her gaze drifted from his face to the mark on his chest. She jerked her head back as though only noticing it for the first time.

"What is that?" she asked, pointing to the cross inside a circle of woven twine.

"A branding. They are popular in some cultures." He did not want to lie to her. But it was too complicated to explain.

"Is it a religious mark?"

Religious? It was the mark of the Devil.

"It is the mark of a wanderer, of a soul lost to the night."

Using the pad of her finger, she traced the outline.

"But you are not lost anymore, Alexander," she said, and he was relieved she had not pressed him for a more definitive explanation. "We have found each other. When you lie awake at night, know that I am also waiting."

Threading his hands into her hair, he guided her mouth to his. The kiss was soft, tender, full of hope. Despite being in a state of semi-arousal—two or three strokes and he could easily have her again—he knew her aunt would be waiting.

"Come, let me help you dress. Your aunt must surely be home and will no doubt be worried."

With wide eyes and a loud gasp she stood up, albeit somewhat awkwardly, and her cheeks flushed a delicate shade of pink. He could smell a trace of blood, had to clench his jaw and grit his teeth for fear of his fangs protracting. Mrs. Shaw's evening repast of animal blood had satisfied his hunger, but the smell of human blood always stirred his senses.

"You'll want to wash," he said, stating the obvious as he stood and helped her rummage around the strewn garments.

She grabbed her petticoat and clutched it to her chest while she searched for her chemise. It was too late for modesty. He'd committed every inch of her body to memory and would spend the daylight hours alone in a candlelit room, sketching her perfect form.

When she located her chemise, he picked up his own garments and dressed quickly before helping her thread her stays and brush the creases from her gown.

Eve threw her hands in the air as she scanned the stained silk. "What on earth will Aunt Beatrice think when she sees me like this?"

Alexander pursed his lips. "I'd worry more about the state of your hair. All you need now is a bundle of rushes, and we could go door to door shouting *chairs to mend.*"

"It's not funny."

"We could always say you fell when Sutherby grabbed you."

She raised a brow. "Although he's a rogue, I will not lie to my aunt."

"Well, we can hardly tell the truth." He stepped closer and straightened the neckline of her gown, purely to satisfy the need to touch her again. "Leave it to me. I can be very persuasive in times of need."

They crept up through the garden; well she crept, Alexander walked behind her at his usual pace. Regardless of what happened or whoever they encountered, they would have no choice but to believe whatever story he told them.

As they passed the ornamental pond Eve suddenly stopped. Without any warning she bent down and thrust her hands into the murky water.

"What on earth are you doing?" he said, unable to hide his surprise or shock when she tipped the contents of her cupped hands over her head.

Rivulets of water ran down her cheeks. Something resembling green sludge clung to the mussed strands of hair.

"I thought I could say it was raining," she said, offering him a weak smile.

Alexander glanced up at the cloudless sky and then back to her bedraggled locks. For the first time in two years, a snigger burst from his lips, and he put his hand to his chest as laughter erupted.

It felt good to release years of suppressed tension. His body became suddenly lighter, and his shoulders dropped an inch. The evil that plagued him was instantly forgotten, and he felt like any other carefree gentleman about his leisure.

Eve laughed, too. He imagined picking her up and swinging her around and around in a bid to prolong the beautiful sound.

"I am half expecting you to jump in," he said.

As her gaze searched his face, her laugh became a warm smile. "You should try laughing more often. When you smile, you look rather dashing."

"It's been a long time since I've had anything to smile about," he said, but then regretted his choice of words as he knew her curious nature would be intrigued by his comment.

Her expression grew solemn. "You speak of your horrendous event in a carriage? Was it an accident?"

Knots formed in his stomach. "Something like that. It was an unfortunate incident. I was the only casualty."

She placed her hand on his arm. "It is all behind you. You must try not to think of it. Terrible things happen to good people every day. As difficult as it may be, you must focus on the here and now."

While he appreciated the words of comfort, it would never be behind him. He would never be free of his affliction.

"I shall heed your wise words." He offered a respectful bow. "I shall focus on the now. At this present moment, we need to get you inside before it rains frogs as well as algae."

They entered the house through the double doors leading into the drawing room. He'd never ravished a lady in her garden or escorted her safely home after the event. Where Evelyn Bromwell was concerned, everything felt new and uncharted.

She put her ear to the door. "I can't hear anything."

He followed her out into the hall, trying not to appear too confident. When they tiptoed past the parlour, she turned to him and breathed a sigh and almost bumped into the maid as she darted around the newel post.

"Goodness, miss. You scared me half to death. Your aunt's just returned. I told her you'd not come home yet."

The maid glanced up at Alexander and then tried her best not to stare at Eve's hair.

"Where is Aunt Beatrice?" Eve whispered.

"She's waiting in the parlour." The maid pointed to the door. "She's been pacing back and forth for the last few minutes. Shall I tell her you're home?"

"No. We're late because we were forced to shelter from the rain." Eve cast Alexander a sidelong glance, the look in her eyes wild and desperate.

"Miss Bromwell is rambling," he said, staring at the maid and focusing on the golden flecks in her brown eyes. "Do you not remember letting us in? You told me to wait in the drawing room almost fifteen minutes ago before you escorted Miss Bromwell upstairs."

The girl looked at him with wide eyes and then blinked rapidly.

"Miss Bromwell is going up to bed." He took Eve's hand

and brought it to his lips. With a discreet flick of the eyes, he gestured to the stairs. "Goodnight, Miss Bromwell. We will discuss the night's events when I see you tomorrow."

"Until tomorrow," she said, offering a coy smile.

He watched her climb the stairs and then turned to the maid. "You should explain your mistake to your mistress."

Without another word, the maid knocked on the door and entered the room opposite.

"Begging your pardon, madam, but I made a mistake. Miss Bromwell is already in her bed, and the gentleman has been waiting in the drawing room for your return."

"Goodness, girl. You said they hadn't arrived home. I've got a good mind to check the decanters. Next, you'll be sleeping in till ten and saying you'd forgotten what time it is."

"Shall I call the gentleman in, madam?"

"Yes, unless you've forgotten how to find your way to the drawing room."

As soon as Alexander stepped over the threshold, Beatrice Penrose rushed to greet him.

"My lord, I cannot thank you enough for coming to my niece's assistance. Lord Markham explained all about Sutherby's appalling antics. Why, the man is a rogue, a veritable scoundrel and not fit for polite society." She gestured to the chairs. "Please, won't you sit down?"

"Indeed." The lady would think him fit for the fiery pits of Hell if she knew of his secret. "It was fortunate for Miss Bromwell that I happened to be passing. I believe the gentleman's affable nature was far from an accurate portrayal of his true character."

"I'm afraid Mr. Sutherby had us all fooled. I am surprised at Lord Foster for recommending him."

Not all, he thought. Alexander had sensed deceit from the moment he'd met him.

"Your friend Lord Markham escorted Mr. Sutherby from the ballroom, discreetly of course, although Miss Sutherby seemed most put out. And you are a hero, my lord. Lord Markham told a lively tale of how you tackled the savage to the ground. In the few short days of our acquaintance, you have saved my life and the reputation of my niece. I assume you were discreet in your attentions?"

"Discreet?" Alexander squirmed in his seat. He did not want praise—not when his thoughts and actions had been purely selfish.

"It wouldn't do to have Evelyn parading around the streets with an unmarried gentleman. Although under the circumstances, I see that there was little option."

"We came the longer route, through the quieter streets and then in through the garden. I assure you, we were not seen. With regard to Mr. Sutherby, I am pleased Miss Bromwell has witnessed the real man hiding behind such a charming facade."

"Who would have thought it?" she said, shaking her head. "He appeared to be so kind, so courteous. And yet at the first opportunity, he thrust his amorous ways on an innocent girl. To think Evelyn had considered marrying him." The woman's gaze drifted over his attire, and she frowned. "Please accept my apologies, my lord, for the poor condition of your clothing. You should send Sutherby the bill for a new shirt and neckcloth."

"It is of no consequence. The pleasure gleaned from such a vigorous activity was payment enough."

Mrs. Penrose shuffled forward in her seat. "I have always enjoyed a good fight, gets the old blood pumping."

Oh, his blood had been pumping.

"I believe any form of exercise is good for the constitution," he replied. "Indeed, I feel better than I have done in years."

"Well, you do appear rather invigorated. Now, we have taken up far too much of your time, my lord. I only hope my niece saw fit to thank you properly."

"She could not have been any more appreciative."

"I dare say, we should put the matter of Mr. Sutherby behind us. Even so, I must admit to being a little disappointed. I have been invited to go to India with Mr. Hartwood. He helped establish a judicial system in Madras and other provinces are eager for his advice and support."

A sudden wave of panic raced through him, gripping him by the throat and squeezing tight.

"India?"

"Mr. Hartwood has asked me to marry him." She clapped her hands together. "I have been a long time widowed and well …"

"Is Miss Bromwell to accompany you on your trip?"

"I haven't mentioned it to her yet. But under the present circumstances, I see no other option. Of course, if she were settled here, then it would be a different matter."

He understood the implication behind the woman's words. But he could not offer marriage, or children, or any sort of future. Guilt, for taking her virginity, flared in his chest. He should have been stronger. He should not have given into the weaknesses of the flesh.

But by God, it had been the most fulfilling moment of his whole damn life.

"We are at home tomorrow if you wish to call for luncheon," Mrs. Penrose said.

"Luncheon? I'm afraid I have a prior engagement. Unless you have no objection to me calling later, for supper perhaps?"

What the hell was he thinking? In his desperation, the words had fallen from his mouth. He could hardly sit with them and eat nothing. He would have to think of an excuse

… perhaps just force down one mouthful, suppress the nausea.

"Supper it is," she said with a smile. "And I'm certain my niece will be desperate to thank you again."

Desire sparked as he thought of all the ways Eve could show her appreciation. "Then I shall look forward to it immensely."

CHAPTER 17

*E*lliot Markham's town residence stood on the west side of Portman Square. The twenty-minute walk from Miss Bromwell's house had given Alexander an opportunity to consider how he wished to approach his friendship with Markham and Devlin.

Friends were untrustworthy.

Neither Reeves nor Lattimer had bothered to search for him after he'd gone missing from the tavern, assuming he'd abandoned them for a pair of cushioned thighs. It was a reasonable assumption, he supposed, but still he had to blame someone.

The difference now was that Markham and Devlin were the only ones to share his secret. They had stated, categorically, that they would never betray a brother, and Alexander could not help but feel a kinship towards them. Despite Markham's arrogance, he'd been more than helpful with Mr. Sutherby and Alexander always paid his dues.

"You took your damn time." Elliot jumped up from his seat in front of the fire in the study. "How long does it take to escort a lady home?"

"I took a detour."

Elliot's curious gaze scanned his attire. "What through a muddy field and a forest full of brambles? Or perhaps a group of wild urchins ripped your shirt in a bid to warm their hands on your bare chest." He chuckled to himself. "Do you want a drink?"

"What are you offering?"

"I was thinking of brandy, but you can have blood if you need it."

"What sort of blood?"

Elliot raised a brow. "Animal, of course. I would always advise against human blood. It's too hard to come by, and you'll only crave it all the more." He moved to the array of decanters lined up on a silver tray.

Alexander strained to look over Elliot's shoulder. "Surely you don't store it in a decanter?"

"It's fine for a few hours," Elliot said as Alexander caught the familiar scent, heard the trickle of what he assumed was brandy. "My footman knows what I like, and I find it a much more gentlemanly ritual."

"Do you not worry he will expose your secret?"

"Not at all. I'm afraid he has the memory of a trout and forgets things easily."

Alexander nodded.

"Here," Elliot said, handing him both glasses. "Try the brandy. It may lighten your mood."

The golden-brown liquid shimmered in the glass. He could not recall the last time he'd drunk anything other than blood.

"You're looking at it as though I distilled it myself in a dank cellar. Try it."

"I haven't eaten or drunk anything in two years. The first time I tried to eat I spewed all over my boots. The stomach cramps were enough to prevent me from attempting it again."

Elliot gestured to the chairs. Alexander drained the glass of animal blood and placed it on the side table before sitting down. He cradled the brandy glass, warming it in his palms as he contemplated lifting it to his lips.

"If you asked Miss Bromwell to drink blood she would retch," Elliot said, throwing himself into the chair opposite. "If she sipped it over a period of time, she would grow accustomed to the taste. I am not saying you won't need blood. You'll need it every day. I am saying it makes it easier if you can appear to enjoy the same pleasures as other gentlemen."

"I have no need to concern myself with appearances. I have no intention of remaining in London."

"What of Miss Bromwell? You have obviously crossed the bounds of propriety. Her scent radiates from you. I find the smell of a woman's sated desire far more potent than blood."

The words roused images of Eve writhing in his lap. In a bid to rein in his rampant thoughts he took a sip of brandy— just enough to wet his lips. It stung the sensitive skin, and he found the sweet aftertaste too overpowering.

"I don't know what to do about Miss Bromwell," he said, surprised that he'd expressed his feelings to a relative stranger. "I almost confided in her tonight. I almost told her what I am."

"I do not think that is wise. Not yet at any rate. Life has a way of revealing the answer to our complex dilemmas when we least expect it. I suggest we concentrate on Mr. Sutherby for the time being."

"We?"

Elliot raised his glass in salute. "We are brothers, Alexander, whether you choose to accept it or not. Your problem is my problem. My secret is safe only as long as yours is, and you would be wise to consider the welfare of both Leo and myself when you make any decisions."

He could not argue with Elliot's logic. "You said we should concentrate on Sutherby. Do you think he will become a nuisance?"

"I know so. What the gentleman says is not what he is thinking. I believe he has convinced himself he is in love with Miss Bromwell. I sense a desperation in him, a conflict. And his sister, well, that is another problem entirely."

Alexander jerked his head back in surprise. "I admit to finding Miss Sutherby somewhat pretentious, but I sensed nothing definable."

"Then I am being overcautious. Just pander to my whims." Elliot sat forward. "Drink up. We need to go."

"Where?"

"To Sutherby's residence. To see what we can discover. Sutherby has undesirable motives, and I'm not convinced he will simply walk away."

Alexander stood and placed his glass on the mantelpiece. "Why should it concern you? Miss Bromwell is my responsibility."

"I'm surprised you need to ask. You're in love with her. If anything should happen to Miss Bromwell, you'll rip the throat out of everyone you meet. That concerns me."

What was the point of protesting? What was the point of denying the truth? He knew he was in love with Evelyn Bromwell. Why else would he have come all the way to town to parade about from ballroom to ballroom?

"Very well. I agree to accompany you to Sutherby's residence. Do you have a plan? Or are we to knock on the door and force them to confess?"

Elliot stood and put a hand on Alexander's shoulder. "Don't worry. We'll find a way in."

∾

They walked the mile to Half Moon Street, the fifteen-minute journey dominated by hilarious tales of Elliot's most recent conquests.

"When she began honking like a goose, I thought I would have to anchor her down for fear she might flap her arms and fly off the bed."

Alexander thought back to his own licentious past. The encounters were meaningless and did nothing to fill the empty void in his chest. Elliot needed to discover the difference between bedding any available woman and bedding a woman he loved.

"I suppose it's preferable to her howling like a dog," Alexander said with a chuckle.

"Not at all. Dogs are far more adventurous with their tongues."

As they passed the turning for Clarges Street, Elliot gripped Alexander's arm, forcing him to stop. "We'll have to go in through the servants' entrance at the front of the house. Sutherby's garden backs directly onto the Clarges Street gardens, and there's no other access."

"And what do we do once we're inside the house?"

"We'll figure that out once we know which room they are in."

Elliot opened the wrought-iron gate, and they descended the stone steps to the basement.

"There's no one in the kitchen," Elliot said, peeking through the window. "It's dark. There are no candles burning. They must all be in bed."

Alexander tried the door to find it locked. "We cannot break down the door. The noise is sure to wake everyone." He glanced at the window, at the row of tiny square glass panes. "If we could get our hand through one of those panes, we could raise the sash."

Elliot examined the window. "Take off your coat. I shall use it as padding to muffle the sound."

"Use your own coat."

Elliot's gaze drifted over him. "Your coat is already crumpled from you earlier liaison. It seems only fair."

With a tut and numerous sighs, Alexander removed his coat and watched as Elliot folded it, pressed it against the glass and used his elbow to shatter the pane.

"Make sure you shake it out before you put it back on," Elliot said with an arrogant smile, "although you're more likely to find a worm crawling inside than a sharp piece of glass."

Contorting his body, Elliot managed to twist his arm through the gap. Once he had pushed the sash up an inch, Alexander gripped the bottom to assist him.

They climbed through the window and stood in the middle of the kitchen.

"Something's wrong here," Elliot said, glancing around the room.

A cold chill hung in the air. They stood in silence and scanned the walls, floor and furniture. Alexander noticed the loaf of bread on a board at the end of the table. He walked over, pulled off a chunk and popped it into his mouth before he could change his mind. It tasted hard, as dry as sawdust. The muscles in his stomach and chest spasmed and he spat it out onto the floor.

"Don't start with bread," Elliot said incredulously. "You need something more moist, something easier to digest. Besides, it looks like that's all they've got to eat."

Alexander walked over to the range, touched the iron door and top plate and peered inside. "It's stone cold. It doesn't look as though there's been a meal prepared in days."

Elliot wandered off down the corridor. Alexander heard him open a door, walk a little further and open another door.

"There are no servants down here," Elliot said, returning to the kitchen. "I doubt there are any in the house."

"Are you certain you have the right address?"

Elliot raised a brow. "I waited for them to leave and followed them home. They hired a hackney as soon as they'd left the square."

"A hackney?"

Alexander recalled the conversation he'd had with the bridle thief at Mytton Grange. Sutherby hadn't paid his servants, and there were no servants at this property, either.

"He's obviously in debt." Elliot glanced up at the ceiling and put his finger to his lips. "Did you hear that?"

Numerous footsteps accompanied the sound of voices drifting down the stairs, the noise getting progressively louder.

"Bloody hell," Alexander whispered. "They're coming down. Quick, close the sash."

Elliot closed the window, wincing as he tried not to make any noise. "Outside," he whispered, pointing to the door.

Alexander unlocked the door and took the key. "I'll lock it from the outside."

They plastered their backs against the wall, each standing on opposite sides of the window. The warm glow flickering against the glass was a sure sign someone had entered the kitchen.

They heard what sounded like pots banging, doors slamming. "What the hell am I supposed to eat? Even the street urchins would turn their noses up at this."

They heard sighs and muttered curses.

"What are you complaining about now?" Miss Sutherby's voice silenced her brother's grumbling.

"There's no food."

Miss Sutherby sighed. "There's bread and fruit and a small chunk of cheese. I'm not a cook. I'm not a maid.

Don't expect me to wander the markets haggling for scraps."

"Bread and cheese? I'd be fed better if I was locked up in Newgate."

"And whose fault is that? Everything would have worked out perfectly if you'd not been so damn careless."

"Me! You're the one who told me to secure a betrothal. One way or another you said."

"Are you stupid? Miss Bromwell is far too intelligent to be won over with amorous kisses and moonlit liaisons."

Alexander couldn't help but form a smug grin. Eve loved nothing more than secret liaisons and passionate kisses—just not with Mr. Sutherby.

"I was desperate. I could have forced the deed had it not been for that devil Hale showing up."

Anger erupted in Alexander's gut. His fingers pulsated as he imagined throttling the man.

Sensing his shift in mood, Elliot shook his head and waved his hands, a gesture to calm a volatile spirit.

"The Earl of Hale obviously has designs on her himself," Miss Sutherby said. "You've seen his estate. It's practically a ruin. I'm sure Miss Bromwell's sizeable inheritance will go a long way to securing his land for future generations."

Elliot gave him a sidelong glance. "Inheritance?" he mouthed.

Alexander shrugged. Although Miss Bromwell and her aunt moved about in Society, they appeared to live quite modestly. They'd hired a carriage to bring them to Mytton Grange and boasted only a handful of servants. Perhaps her inheritance was payable upon marriage.

"Hale is interested in more than her money. I've seen the way he looks at her. I mean she's damnably pretty and always pleasant company."

"I knew it," Miss Sutherby exclaimed. "You've developed

a liking for her. I've seen it in your eyes when you speak to her."

"I have not."

"You believe yourself in love with her."

"I do not. Now you're being ridiculous."

"If you think you're going to marry her and not share the money with me, then you can think again. I know enough to see you hang."

"Miss Bromwell will not want to marry me now," Mr. Sutherby complained. "Not after the debacle in the garden."

"Well, you had better hope she does. We owe rent on this house and at Mytton Grange, not to mention the bill for the modiste, the tailors—"

"Perhaps we should just leave here and move on. What about York or Edinburgh?"

"Move on!" Miss Sutherby shrieked. "You were not the one who had to fawn over portly lords to gain invitations. It will take months to find another heiress. What are we supposed to eat in the meantime, Scotch mist? You really do say the most pathetic things."

"Why do you always treat me like a child? You take your role of sibling far too seriously."

"One of us has to take control else we'll end up in debtors' prison."

"Miss Bromwell never treats me like an idiot. She always smiles and nods and offers witty remarks. Perhaps I should just leave you and take my chances. You won't say a thing. If I hang, so will you."

"You ... you know you don't mean that." There was a nervous edge to her tone. "Miss Bromwell may smile and laugh, but she is a respectable lady, full of purity and virtue. You know she cannot give you what you want. She will run away from you like a frightened little kitten, hide in the corner mewling and licking her paws."

143

The woman did not know Miss Bromwell very well at all.

"Then perhaps you should remember that you need me," he said. "Without me, none of this would be possible. Perhaps you should start being a little kinder, more appreciative."

"If you want kindness," she said with a slow purr, "you shall have it."

The room fell silent.

Alexander glanced at Elliot, who threw his hands up and offered a shrug.

They heard a scraping sound: wood against the tiled floor, then a dull thud accompanied by Mr. Sutherby's deep groan. Curiosity burning, Alexander couldn't help but sneak a glance through the window.

Sutherby was leaning back against the crude table, his breeches bunched around his ankles while his sister took him in hand.

"Oh, God, Julia," he panted as she dropped to her knees. "This is why I love you."

Julia?

Alexander shot back against the wall, his eyes wide, his mouth hanging open.

"What is it?" Elliot whispered.

"Take a look for yourself."

Elliot peeked through the window and remained there for longer than was necessary. "I could find a use for a mouth like that," he said, moving back to the wall.

"We'll have to wait here until they've finished."

"Take me, Henry, take me now."

Henry?

"Sorry, but I'm going to have to have another look," Elliot said with a grin.

"What's happening?"

"He's taking her over the table. They'll need to slow

down otherwise the only bit of bread they've got will be cata-pulted into the air."

"Shush, before they hear you."

"They won't hear us over the grunts and groans. If only I had a sister like that."

Alexander sighed. "I think it is fair to assume she is not his sister."

"Agreed. I bet she's fair game, though."

Alexander glared at him. "They intend to hurt Miss Bromwell. So much for your loyalty to the brotherhood."

"I was thinking of you. I could punish her severely until she begs me to stop."

"Are there no limits to your depravity?"

"No." Elliot sighed. "We all have our way of coping with the cards dealt us. But you know I speak in jest. You know I would never betray a brother."

"Good," Alexander said, "as we can't take the chance of being caught here, not with just hours until dawn. I will inform Miss Bromwell tomorrow night and then we will return and confront them."

"Very well."

"Make sure you get all the sustenance you need before we come back. I will need you to be focused."

Elliot smirked. "You're worried I might drink from them?"

"When I said sustenance, I wasn't talking about blood."

CHAPTER 18

They walked as far as Clarges Street and Alexander suddenly stopped. "Perhaps I should call on Miss Bromwell. Her house is a few minutes from here. I'll tell her what we've discovered about the Sutherbys."

Elliot smirked. "Are you certain that's the only reason you wish to call? Perhaps the sight of the Sutherbys' amorous display has left you craving a certain form of stimulation. I know I won't be going straight home." He jerked his head up to the night sky. "You do not have long until dawn, so you'll need to be quick. Mind you don't get too distracted."

Alexander nodded. "I'll call on you tomorrow evening, and we'll decide what to do about Sutherby."

Elliot was right. Telling Eve about Sutherby was not the only reason for his visit. After their interlude in the garden, he was desperate to see her, to know she was well, to know she had no regrets. This craving that consumed him was like a delicious form of madness. The few hours since their separation felt like days. If he hurried, he'd have time to make it home before the sun's scalding rays singed his skin.

Following the route through the mews, he entered her

garden and sat down beneath the cherry tree before focusing his thoughts and calling out to her. If her revelation about struggling to sleep was true, he knew his silent endearments would rouse her easily.

While he waited, he stared up into the darkness. The memory of his first night as a monster came back to haunt him.

The images always came as fragments, like the jumbled parts of a torn picture, brief flashes that had taken time to piece together.

He remembered lying on the bed, the vixen's sharp fangs piercing his skin. A coldness enveloped him. He woke to find himself lying on the forest floor. Glancing down at his attire, he realised he was wearing the same clothes he'd worn in the tavern, had almost laughed at the thought it had all been a drunken dream.

But his dream soon turned into a nightmare.

The clawing pangs of hunger refused to be tempered, and he'd stumbled towards the road in search of help. A man driving a cart stopped to offer assistance, berated him for wandering the woods at night when wolves roamed aplenty. He'd offered to take him to the nearest village, assumed he was just another rich lord, lost after an evening of bawdy pleasure.

Oh, he *was* lost—lost to the night that had so cruelly claimed him.

Even in the dark, Alexander could see the vein in the peasant's neck pulse. As he sat next to him on the crude seat, he stared at it, transfixed by the rhythmical throbbing. The sound mimicked the ticking of a clock. Each beat, each passing second, drawing him closer until his teeth ached— until they protruded further from his gums.

He drank from the man while he lay writhing and scream- ing, spewed the first mouthful of blood before it had hit his stomach. Thankfully, he'd stopped before any lasting damage was done.

And so a monster was born.

He'd never drunk from another human, sworn he never would.

"This is a surprise." Eve's soft voice penetrated the nightmare.

Alexander stood abruptly, shook his head and focused on the vision of beauty before him. "You heard my call," he said, trying to suppress the feeling of melancholy that always accompanied painful memories. "I wasn't sure you'd come."

Without a word, she ran into his arms. He hugged her tightly, kissed the top of her head as a way of soothing his own sorry soul.

"I heard your voice, and it brought me here," she said, cuddling into him. She felt warm, smelled of clean linen and rosewater.

"After what happened between us, I wanted to check you were all right."

It was the first time in his life he had given a damn.

She looked up at him and smiled. "Do not feel as though you have taken advantage of me. Everything that has occurred between us has happened because I wanted it to."

The warmth in his chest journeyed south towards his groin. He wondered how he would cope if she walked away from him. With every ounce of his being, he wanted to tell her what she meant to him, but the fear of rejection loomed large. What future was there for her? He should tell her his secret, but he could not bear to talk about it tonight, not after reliving his nightmare. Not when he felt so akin to the monster inside.

With nothing to say, he chose to pour his heart into a kiss that was deep and tender. He kissed her as though he was dying and the touch of her lips was to be his lasting memory.

He kissed her as though he had waited a thousand years for the pleasure.

The urge to thrust inside was soon upon him, and he broke away with a muttered curse.

"What's wrong?" she asked, her expression revealing a level of anxiety he'd not seen before. He knew then that he couldn't tell her the truth about Sutherby. Not yet, at least.

"Desire burns inside me," he confessed. "The need to have you is overwhelming."

She seemed pleased, his answer causing her to reveal her own desire as she pressed her body closer and ran her hands up over his chest.

"It's too soon," he continued, as he listened to the lascivious train of her thoughts. Yet in truth, it felt like an eternity since he'd joined with her. "I don't want to hurt you."

"You keep saying that," she said with a giggle. "I know you would never hurt me."

"Let us sit under the tree. Let me hold you in my arms. Tell me something you have never told another."

She tilted her head, her gaze curious and he had to admit he did not sound like himself. Ignoring his suggestion, she took his hand and pulled him down. Bunching her nightgown up past her thighs she straddled him, taking him by surprise. "I'm sitting," she said with a coy smile. "I want to be with you, Alexander. Nothing else matters."

Everything else mattered.

But he would leave her to enjoy one more night in blissful ignorance.

When he glanced down, the sight of her bare thighs gripping him was his undoing. He would have one more night, too. A night to bask in her beauty. A night to forget his troubles. With eager fingers, he unbuttoned his breeches and pushed home.

She took the length of him with a pleasurable hum,

moving the way he'd taught her just a few hours earlier. The ripples of pure pleasure made his soul soar, and he committed the feeling to memory.

As he sucked in a ragged breath, he glanced up at the night sky. The varying shades of grey were an ominous warning. Time was slipping away. He was in danger of being lost in the moment, and he gripped her hips to quicken the pace. Sitting up to wrap his arm around her waist, he rained kissed along her collarbone, claimed her mouth in a mad frenzy as he helped her to pump him quickly.

Their release came like a bolt from the heavens: swift and sudden, their bodies jerking violently in response. She held on to him as her shudders subsided and he imagined lying with her in bed, holding her close until the night came again.

"I should go," he said, knowing he would have to run through the streets to make it home before sunrise. Yet still he struggled to free himself from her warm body.

When they had fixed their clothing, he offered a chaste kiss. "You should hurry before someone sees you. I'll wait until you're safely inside."

She stood on her tiptoes and kissed him again. "Will I still see you tomorrow?"

"You mean today," he said with a weak smile, brushing her hair from her face. "Yes. There are many things we need to discuss."

CHAPTER 19

*T*he thin rays of dawn found a way through the gaps
in the curtains, the hazy slivers of light coming to
rest on Evelyn's bed. She'd not slept since Alexander had left
but only drifted in and out of whimsical daydreams.
Conjuring fanciful musings of Alexander Cole was the next
best thing to being held in his arms.

She had often imagined a love so deep it would make her
heart ache. The reality was a feeling of intense euphoria
infused with a gut-wrenching pain brought about by even the
shortest separation. Now she understood why losing one's
true love caused many people to drink themselves into
oblivion.

When one truly loved someone, there was no need to sit
and think and examine one's feelings. True love brought a
level of acceptance—she felt the truth of it deep in her core,
and nothing could ever change it. All those hours spent
pondering over a match with Mr. Sutherby, dredging up every
logical reason why she should accept, had all been in vain.
Even if she'd tried, she could never have loved him like she
loved Alexander.

The thought of Mr. Sutherby's clammy hands caressing her body made her shiver. She jumped out of bed, threw back the curtains and picked up her book from the nightstand. A few hours reading, a late breakfast and by the time she'd washed, dressed and daydreamed a little more, the hours would soon pass.

There are many things we need to discuss.

Her stomach flipped over when she recalled Alexander's words. The earliest she imagined him calling was two. It was only hours away, yet it felt like weeks, months.

Evelyn read a few pages of her book before her mind drifted back to Alexander. Perhaps she should have borrowed Hatton's *Secrets in Every Mansion* in the hope the novel would offer insight into why he had locked himself away at Stony Cross. He had tried to tell her his secret last night, but she'd wanted him to know she loved him unconditionally and wanted nothing to distract from the moment.

Perhaps he had an illegitimate child, but that would hardly prevent him from embracing Society. Perhaps he was the one responsible for the terrible carriage accident, and the only way to cope with the guilt was to live the life of a recluse. Perhaps he was debt-ridden and had no other choice but to be frugal. Considering the dilapidated condition of his estate and his paltry pantry, the last option sounded the most feasible.

With the tip of her finger, she scanned the page looking for a familiar sentence so she could continue reading. After a few more pages impatience prevailed, and she decided not to wait for Katie's morning call.

When she walked into the dining room wearing her night-gown and wrapper, her aunt's lower lip almost hit the table.

"Evelyn. What are you doing down so early? It must only be eight o'clock."

"I couldn't sleep." She walked over to the sideboard,

picked up a plate and lifted the lid on the silver serving dish. The smell of bacon wafted up to tease her nostrils. Her stomach groaned in appreciation. The early morning activities had left her famished. "I've been wide awake for hours and my mind was too distracted to read."

"Oh, dear. Is it that terrible business in the garden?"

Evelyn's heart skipped a beat, maybe two or three. Surely her aunt did not know of her liaisons with Alexander, although such magnificent moments could hardly be described as terrible.

"It's lucky Lord Hale happened to walk by," her aunt continued, "else heaven only knows what devious plans Mr. Sutherby had in mind for you. And to think I thought he was such an affable gentleman and even encouraged the match."

"You were not to know," Evelyn said, sitting down opposite her aunt, desperate to tuck into the plate of eggs and bacon. "Mr. Sutherby fooled us all."

"He certainly did," she replied with a firm nod. "There's warm toast in the rack."

Evelyn took a piece and covered it with a thin layer of butter. "I wonder if Mr. Sutherby told Charlotte what happened last night."

"Lord Markham took her to one side and informed her that her brother needed to leave. I assume she'd be mortified if she knew of his sinful urges and lustful cravings. Such a quiet, elegant young lady."

"I don't suppose she'll be pleased when she discovers we're no longer destined to be sisters. She's talked of nothing else all week."

"Yes. She did seem desperate to see her brother wed." Aunt Beatrice patted Evelyn's hand. "I hope you're not too disappointed. I had hoped to see you happy and settled but …"

"There's plenty of time," Evelyn said, trying not to show

her relief at having an excuse to refuse the match. "I have a few years before I'll be considered unmarriageable."

"I just don't like to see you upset."

"I'm fine." *Fine* didn't even begin to describe how wonderful she felt.

"Never mind. Our trip to India will take your mind off it and give you something else to focus on. You never know, you may meet a wealthy merchant who's desperate for an English wife."

Evelyn practically choked on her tea. "Our trip to India?"

"I knew you'd be surprised," her aunt said, clasping her hands to her chest. "Mr. Hartwood has asked me to marry him. He wants us to go to India, only for six months or so. Can you believe it? After all these years. Your mother always said I should have married Mr. Hartwood, but we were young, and our parents did not approve."

"You're to be married?"

"Yes." Her aunt beamed. "You have no idea what went through my mind as I lay dying in the wreckage. I thought of all the things I would miss, thought of all the things I'd regret. It forced me to accept what I have spent years denying."

Evelyn struggled with a range of conflicting emotions. "That's wonderful, Aunt Bea. I'm so happy for you," she said, feigning a smile. The muscles in her stomach twisted into painful knots. She felt nauseous and light-headed at the prospect of leaving Alexander. "Isn't it a little sudden, though?"

"Sudden?" her aunt repeated as her eyes widened. "I have always loved Mr. Hartwood and have waited more than thirty years for a second chance at happiness."

Happiness? What of her happiness? Was this to be the end of everything?

"Are you sure you want to leave your home?" Evelyn

hoped her words sounded sincere, hoped her concerns sounded genuine.

It took all her effort not to jump from the chair and shout and scream at her aunt for her selfishness. But it was wrong of her to feel that way. Her aunt had been her guardian for the last five years and had always put her needs first.

"That reminds me. I'm to meet Mr. Hartwood this afternoon. He is taking me to see the *Camellia Japonica* exhibit at Vauxhall. The Chandler and Buckingham Nursery are desperate to show their exotic flowers now they're in full bloom. You're welcome to join us. We'll be back in plenty of time to take supper with Lord Hale."

"Supper? Lord Hale is coming for supper?"

Could the day hold any more surprises?

She'd have to wait another twelve hours to see him again. At the present moment, twelve hours was a mere trifle when compared to being separated by thousands of miles.

"I invited him last night. It is the least we can do after he took the trouble to escort you home and in such a discreet manner." Her aunt took a sip of her tea. "He does seem somewhat protective of you. There are few gentlemen who would act so selflessly. I believe he is of a mind to wed and thinks you a possible match."

An array of heavenly images flashed through Evelyn's mind, pictures of wedded bliss. They were running around the fountain at Stony Cross, laughing and flicking water over one another. They were lying on the lush green lawn surrounded by vibrant rose blooms, his body pressing down on hers as they frolicked under the heat of the midday sun.

Evelyn swallowed deeply.

She'd always professed to be a realist. Yet now her mind was possessed by romantic visions, her heart plagued by fantasies of everlasting love.

"I think your own excitement has affected your judgement, Aunt Bea. Lord Hale is far too complex a man to be defined by the usual modes of conduct." She wiped her mouth with her napkin and stood. "I think I'll go upstairs and read before I take my bath."

"Are you coming to Vauxhall? It would give you a chance to get to know Mr. Hartwood a little better."

"Thank you, but I think I'll stay here. Perhaps you should invite Mr. Hartwood to dinner tomorrow."

"What a wonderful idea." Aunt Beatrice's smile faded. "I hope you're not coming down with a chill after being outdoors for so long last night. No doubt a good soak in a warm bathtub will do you the power of good."

"I'm sure it will." To be held tightly against a warm chest would serve her better, Evelyn thought, as she left the room.

So much for a soak in a hot bath. The water was cold by the time Katie came back in, and Evelyn wished she'd bathed in a chemise.

"Sorry, miss, I know I was supposed to bring the kettle, but there's a letter come for you," the maid said from behind the screen. "The boy wouldn't hand it over, not until we'd given him something to eat. He ate two whole servings of Mrs. Anderson's broth and still I had to grab it from his mucky fingers."

Katie's hand appeared around the screen, waving a linen towel for Evelyn to dry her hands before offering the letter.

Evelyn resisted the urge to snatch it from her grasp. Despite her tummy performing somersaults, she turned it over but found no evidence of Alexander's seal pressed into the wax. Not that she'd expected to see the mark. It would be unwise to reveal his identity when sending such a private missive.

"Did the boy say who sent it?"

"No, miss. Just that a gentleman paid him to deliver it. A nabob he said."

Her stomach flipped over again as she broke the seal.

Evelyn scanned the elegant script, her eyes racing to the bottom and widening when she noticed it had been signed with one strong, masculine word: *Hale*. With her heart all aflutter she read the contents.

I hope this letter finds you well after the incident in the garden ...

Incident! The word sounded so cold and unfeeling. Had he not felt the same burning desire? Could he not have thought of a better way to express himself? Perhaps he struggled to convey what he felt in his heart or feared someone else might read it. Thankfully, his tone improved as she read on.

I know how you like to walk outside in the moonlight ...

Now he was teasing her.

Perhaps you would care to join me at the Forbes' exhibition. The gallery is displaying an assortment of paintings and the theme is "moonlight" ...

It was a rather romantic gesture, and so she could forgive him for his earlier mishap.

We shall have the gallery to ourselves and may peruse them at our leisure. Discretion is paramount. I shall send a carriage for you at three. Wait on the corner of Ryder and Bury Street.

No doubt he would wait inside the exhibition. He must have paid Forbes handsomely for the privilege, and it put into question her earlier assumption that he was debt-ridden. He obviously still kept a carriage in town despite insisting he never rode in one.

"The boy's waiting for your reply, miss," Katie said, disturbing her reverie.

"Oh, yes." She glanced down at the water. It would take her an age to get dry. "Just tell the boy I am in agreement. There's no need to say anything more."

"Very well, miss," the maid said, and Evelyn heard her pad across the floor and leave the room.

Evelyn read the letter again. Had she not been so wet, she would have hugged it to her chest. At least she would not have to wait until supper to see him and being alone with him would mean more sinful gazes and amorous kisses.

Katie came back to help her out of the tub, and once she was dry, she popped on a wrapper.

"Your aunt said she's leaving at one and will have luncheon out. Will you be coming down to eat or shall I bring something up?"

That would leave Evelyn two hours to get ready before Alexander's carriage came. She could say she was going to read in the garden. No one would bother to check on her.

"No. After such a filling breakfast, I couldn't manage anything else to eat." Besides, nerves had caused her to lose her appetite.

"Well, just ring if you change your mind."

"I might go out into the garden to read. It's such a nice day. I'll wear a long-sleeved walking dress just in case it gets cold."

The maid didn't question her choice, and Evelyn didn't mention wearing the yellow spencer.

Just before three o'clock, she went out into the garden with both her book and a blanket in hand. The blanket disguised her jacket, and she draped it over her arm until she reached the cherry tree.

Memories of their illicit encounters came flooding back. The image of Alexander sitting beneath the tree caused desire to unfurl. If she closed her eyes, she could smell his earthy, masculine scent. She could hear his ragged breath, almost feel it breezing against her skin. The combination heightened the need to see him, to touch him, and she practically threw the blanket and book on the ground to fasten her jacket.

Checking over her shoulder, she snuck out through the mews and hurried along the pavement towards the unmarked carriage waiting near the corner of Bury Street.

Upon witnessing her approach, the coachman lowered his head. "Are you here for the Earl of Hale?" he said, jowls of fatty flesh wobbling as he spoke.

Evelyn nodded, and the man climbed down, his heavy frame blocking the entrance as he opened the carriage door and lowered the steps. Moving to the right, he held his hand out and gestured inside.

With the carriage blinds drawn the interior appeared darker than she was expecting. It was then she noticed the pair of black Hessian boots.

"Alexander?" she said, mounting the last step and ducking through the door. "I expected you to wait at the gallery. I thought you said you refused to—oomph!"

The coachman pushed her inside, threw up the steps and slammed the door.

"Alexander. What on earth is going on?"

Evelyn felt a hand at her elbow as the occupant helped her to her seat. The carriage lurched forward, and the gentleman raised the blind before removing his top hat.

"Forgive my heavy-handedness, Miss Bromwell, but I'm afraid you left me with no other choice."

"Mr. Sutherby!"

CHAPTER 20

*A*lexander rode through the streets as though the buildings were about to come crashing down around him. Carriages swerved to avoid him; the irate curses and loud jeering did not deter him from his course. He almost trampled over a man pushing his knife-sharpening cart.

Please hurry, Alexander! Please find me.

The words echoed through his mind once more, rebounding back to cause a sharp pain in his heart. The plea sounded desperate, yet oddly calm. He didn't know what the hell to make of it. Beads of perspiration trickled down his brow. Every muscle in his body felt hard, taut. Panic flared again, restricting his airways as he struggled to shake the feeling that something disastrous had happened.

Fearing there was no time to ride round to the mews, he tethered his horse to the railings outside Evelyn's house and vaulted the few steps leading up to the front door.

His incessant banging produced the desired effect as the butler's heels clipped at a hurried pace towards the door.

"I need to speak to Miss Bromwell," he said, thrusting his

hat at the man as he barged through the door. "I must speak to her now."

"I am afraid she is not at home."

"Who is it, Radley? Who's there? Is it Evelyn?"

Beatrice Penrose came darting out into the hall. She looked tired and weary. The red marks beneath her lower lids suggested she'd been weeping, and her anxious gaze sent a frisson of fear shooting straight through him.

"Lord Hale," she gasped rushing forward to take his hand. The overfamiliar gesture confirmed his suspicion. "Tell me my niece is with you. Tell me this has all been a terrible misunderstanding."

Alexander swallowed deeply as she released her grip. His throat felt dry as he tried to form the words. "You mean, Miss Bromwell is not here?"

Mrs. Penrose shook her head and dabbed at the corner of her eyes with her handkerchief. "No, my lord. She has been missing for hours."

"Missing? How can she be missing?" he said, his tone revealing his anger and frustration at such utter incompetence.

"One minute she was in the garden reading, the next she had disappeared. She left her book and blanket under the cherry tree. We've searched the whole house."

There had to be an explanation.

"What time was this?" he asked, pulling out his watch. He'd heard the first call from her at about four, some three hours ago. Luckily, the thick blanket of cloud acted as a barrier to the sun's powerful rays but still he'd been forced to wait and pace the floor for hours until the sun had almost set.

"Her maid said she went out into the garden just before three. No one thought to check on her, not in her own garden."

"And now it's seven," he muttered to himself. "Did she

have any plans for the evening ... dinner or the theatre, perhaps?"

Mrs. Penrose frowned. "But we were to take supper with you, my lord. Don't you remember?"

"Yes, of course." He dragged his hand down his face and sighed. "Did she give any indication she had made any plans for the afternoon, perhaps with friends?"

"No. I invited her to Vauxhall, but she said she was going to have a warm bath. I was worried she'd caught a chill."

Guilt flared as he recalled the cool night air breezing over her naked body.

"If she was out in the garden perhaps someone saw her leaving through the mews," he said, still feeling like the worst of rogues.

"Why would she leave the house without telling anyone? She's never done anything like this before."

"Begging your pardon, madam," the maid said, stepping forward from the shadows. "But it might have something to do with the letter she received."

"Letter?" Mrs. Penrose screeched. "What letter?"

The maid curtsied. "I never mentioned it before, madam, what with it being a private matter. A boy delivered it and waited for a reply." The girl sniffed and her bottom lip quivered. "I didn't want to cause Miss Bromwell any trouble."

"And you did not think it worth our attention?" Mrs. Penrose tutted. But on witnessing the girl's distress, patted her on the shoulder. "Never mind, Katie. You were not to know."

"Where is this letter?" Alexander asked.

"It might be in her room, my lord."

Mrs. Penrose threw her arms in the air. "Well, go and get it. Under the circumstances, I'm sure she'll understand the need to forgo privacy."

The maid bunched her skirt and raced up the stairs before

returning promptly, flapping the paper with delight as though waving a flag at a royal procession.

Mrs. Penrose unfolded the paper and proceeded to read the note. She stopped, looked up at him and narrowed her gaze.

"What is the meaning of this, my lord?" she said, not bothering to hide her displeasure. "How can you stand there and feign ignorance?"

What the blazes was she talking about?

Alexander snatched the letter from her hand and ignored her shriek and look of horror. His gaze darted to his name signed fraudulently at the bottom of the missive.

"Bloody hell," he said, unable to suppress his frustration as he continued reading. He silenced her aunt's muttered objection by raising his hand.

"Well?" she asked when he'd finally finished. "What have you to say?"

"I can assure you, Mrs. Penrose, I did not write this letter," he said, almost thrusting it in her face. "Why would I need to see Miss Bromwell when you had already invited me to supper? As I mentioned last night, I had a prior engagement and could not possibly have met with her today."

"Then what dastardly deed is this, my lord?" she implored. "And if you're ignorant of it, why arrive here as if the Devil were chasing your heels?"

What the hell was he supposed to say? He could hardly tell the woman that he'd heard her niece calling to him by way of a silent plea. That no matter where she was, he was connected to her now—for always. Forever.

"Because I have recently discovered the depth of Mr. Sutherby's deviousness," he said, angry with himself for not mentioning it to Eve when he had the chance. "The gentleman has no money and cannot pay the rent on any of the properties he's leased. His creditors are all but hammering on his door, hence his intention to marry Miss Bromwell and claim her sizeable inheritance." He chose not to divulge the truth behind Sutherby's relationship with Charlotte or whatever her blasted name was. "Hence his bid to compromise her in the garden."

Mrs. Penrose stared at him, her mouth hanging open. "But there is no inheritance. I mean, Evelyn has an income of a few hundred pounds a year, but she received it immediately upon her parents' deaths. She will inherit nothing more when she marries. The manor and all the surrounding land was entailed."

Alexander brushed his hand through his hair and scratched his head. "Then why does Sutherby think she's an heiress?"

"I have no idea."

"Well, Sutherby must have written the letter. He is the only other person, other than Lord Markham, who knows what happened in the garden last night."

"But what would he hope to achieve by it? Do you think he intends to demand a ransom?"

Alexander had no idea what the man was capable of. But the longer he stood conversing with her aunt, the longer Eve was alone with Sutherby.

"Whatever Sutherby's plan, you must trust me to find your niece and bring her home safely. I would like to keep the letter if I may."

Mrs. Penrose nodded. "You have saved us both on occasion, my lord, and I trust you will come to her rescue again."

"I assure you, I will not return without her," he said, grabbing his hat before heading out of the door.

Mounting his horse, Alexander's first thought was to ride directly to Sutherby's house on Half Moon Street, although the man would have to be an idiot to take Evelyn somewhere so close to home. Sutherby must have hired the carriage he used to transport Evelyn to some unknown destination. With his finances in such a sorry state, the act was a sure sign of desperation.

And desperate men did desperate things.

An image of Evelyn lying bound and gagged flashed through his mind, and he clenched his jaw as he dug his heels in and raced towards Elliot's house in Portman Square.

When he eventually found Evelyn, he would need a carriage to bring her home. When he found her, he would need someone to stop him from ripping the scoundrel's throat out.

As Alexander rode into Portman Square, he found Elliot standing on the pavement next to his carriage, examining his pocket watch beneath the light of the lamp. He looked up and gave Alexander a nod before dismissing the liveried footmen. With numerous gestures to the crest on the door, his coachman climbed down from his box.

"I need your help," Alexander panted, not bothering to jump down from his horse. He glanced at the carriage. "You're not going out?"

"I've been waiting," Elliot said, replacing his watch. "I knew you'd come. And the only place I'm going tonight is with you."

The coachman rolled out two pieces of cloth with metal brackets sewn onto the ends and proceeded to cover Markham's crest by clipping them onto the doors.

"How did you know I'd be coming?"

Elliot threw his hands up and shrugged. "Usually, I struggle to hear people's thoughts when I'm not in the immediate vicinity. But for some bizarre reason, I could feel your pain. I've been pacing for the last hour, wondering what the hell was going on. I told Gibbs to ready my carriage, yet I have no notion where we are going."

"Miss Bromwell is missing." Alexander steadied his

horse, the animal sensing his agitation. "She received a note, supposedly signed by my hand."

"But you think it was Sutherby."

"Who else? I should have put an end to all of this last night."

Elliot smirked. "You mean you did not tell Miss Bromwell the news when you called on her again?"

"Well, no." He was an idiot, a selfish fool. He reached into his coat pocket and removed the letter. "Here, read this."

There was a moment of silence before Elliot blurted, "But she met him almost five hours ago." The trace of panic in his voice hit Alexander like a hard blow to the stomach. "They could be anywhere. On the road to Scotland, heading towards the south coast … anywhere."

The blood drained from Alexander's face. Finding them would be an impossible task. He knew that. But he would just have to follow his instincts.

"I'll meet you at Sutherby's house on Half Moon Street," Alexander said, folding the letter and putting it back in his pocket. "I doubt he'll have taken her there, but we may find some clue as to his intention."

Elliot nodded. "Very well. I think we know his motivation is money. He'll not harm her, not when he sees her as a commodity."

"Am I supposed to feel reassured?"

"We'll find her," Elliot said firmly. He glanced at Alexander's horse. "I'll call a boy to stable your horse."

"That won't be necessary. I prefer to ride."

"What's the matter? Frightened I might bite you?"

The words were said in jest, yet he felt a frisson of fear at the memory of the devil woman's closed carriage, fear that quickly turned to anger. "In my haste to find Miss Bromwell, I've not sated my hunger this evening. There's every chance

I'd drain you dry. Now, shut the hell up and follow me to Sutherby's."

They entered the house using the same method as the previous night. As they stood in the kitchen, the image of Sutherby's naked buttocks balancing on the edge of the table flashed into his mind, and he kicked the blasted thing in a bid to release his frustration.

"Be quiet," Elliot whispered, hitting him on the arm.

"Why?"

"What if you're wrong, and Sutherby comes down and finds us in here? Despite covering my crest, someone will have noticed us arriving."

"I'm not wrong, and I don't give a damn who notices."

Alexander stomped off through the basement and climbed the stairs to the ground floor. He was rummaging through the desk in the study when Elliot entered.

"Other than an old newspaper, there's nothing in any of the rooms down here. They feel cold and desolate as though no one has lived here for months. Did you find anything of interest in here?"

"Not a blasted thing. All the drawers were open. I found some letters, but nothing relating to Sutherby. If that's even his name."

Elliot folded his arms across his chest. "Did Sutherby have any friends here in town? Perhaps we could find them and torture them for information."

Alexander shook his head. "Not that I know of." He was not averse to torture, not where Sutherby was concerned. "I've only ever seen him with his sister, or his lover or whoever the hell she is."

"At least we know Miss Bromwell is not here. I do not feel any remnants of her presence. But then you would be the better judge of that." Elliot paused, narrowed his gaze and glanced up at the ceiling. "However, I believe someone is here. Listen."

Alexander stared at a point in the far corner of the room as he honed his senses. The faint melody resonated through the house: high-pitched humming accompanied by the odd string of words. The country tune was barely audible, and he crept over to Elliot and led him to the bottom of the stairs.

"It's coming from the room above the study," he whispered, jabbing his finger up and to the left.

"Sounds like a woman's voice," Elliot said, moving up a few steps and peering through the balusters. "The chamber door is closed."

Climbing stealthily to the top, they padded across the landing to stand outside the door.

It was definitely a woman, although she sounded far too cheerful to be Evelyn. They listened for a moment but heard no one else.

"Perhaps it's Charlotte Sutherby?" Elliot whispered.

They heard splashing and the slow trickle of water. Elliot's hand hovered over the door handle.

Alexander grabbed his wrist. "Wait. If I … if I lose control, I need you to stop me. If you see my eyes darken. If you see me flex my jaw …"

Elliot smiled. "Trust me. Based on what I expect to find beyond this door, I believe I'll be the one losing control. If you see me unbutton my breeches, then you'll know it's time to act."

CHAPTER 21

*A*lexander followed Elliot into the room. He wasn't sure what he expected to find, but instinct told him it wouldn't be Evelyn. The shocking sight caused them both to stop abruptly.

"You took your time," Charlotte Sutherby said. She was standing in a small tin bath with her back to them. Her honey-gold hair was draped over one shoulder as she massaged soap all over her naked body.

The scene left him cold, but he could hear the wild, chaotic train of Elliot's thoughts. Feeling tension emanate from his friend's body, he could only imagine his physical reaction to the enticing vision.

The lady bent down and swished her cloth in the water before wringing it out over her neck and shoulders, offering a pleasurable hum at the sensation. In the muted light, her silhouette appeared softer, her skin bathed in a peachy-cream glow.

"Bloody hell," Elliot whispered.

"Well?" she said. "Did you do what I asked? Did you call on Miss Bromwell and offer an apology?"

When neither of them answered, she glanced casually over her shoulder. The ear-piercing shriek made him wince, and the woman almost fell out of the tub in shock.

"What … what the hell are you doing in here? How did you get in?" After numerous failed attempts to use her arms to protect her modesty, she crouched down. Her frantic gaze darted to the garment hanging on the door of the armoire. "Get out! Get out, I said."

"I'm afraid that won't be possible." Elliot strode over to the crude wooden chair in the corner of the room and moved it to the other side of the tub. Flicking out the tails of his coat, he sat down and continued to admire the view. "Not until you've told us everything you know."

"Know? About what?"

Despite feeling like a randy schoolboy peeping on his maid, Alexander stepped closer. "Sutherby has left. He isn't coming back."

When she shot up and swung around with a gasp, Elliot sucked in a breath. "You appear to be suffering from the cold. Shall I heat more water?"

She ducked down again. "What do you mean, he's not coming back?"

Alexander gritted his teeth. "We have not come here to answer your questions."

"Sorry to be the bearer of bad news," Elliot said, crossing his legs out in front of him. "But your gentleman friend has kidnapped Miss Bromwell."

Her gazed darted back and forth between them. "Kidnapped her? With what? A hawker's barrow?" Clutching her arms to her chest, she turned to Elliot and wiggled her fingers at the armoire. "Hand me my wrapper."

"In a moment." A lascivious grin played at the corners of Elliot's mouth. "You'll get your wrapper when you've told us what we need to know … Julia."

She gasped, her eyes wide and fearful. "How … how do you know?"

"We're wasting time," Alexander said, suppressing the feeling of hopelessness. As the minutes ticked by, Evelyn slipped further and further away from him. If he lost her, he'd have nothing left. He marched over to the tub, ignoring Miss Sutherby's state of undress. "Where the hell has he taken her?"

She shook her head. "I don't know. I don't know what you're talking about."

"Sutherby, or Henry or whatever his blasted name is, has tricked Miss Bromwell into thinking she was meeting me. She climbed into a carriage with him at three and has not been seen since."

Her face turned pale, ashen and her bottom lip almost hit the water. After a brief moment of silence, her wide eyes narrowed, and she jumped up from her bath like Poseidon charging out of the sea.

With no thought to her modesty, she thrust her hands on her hips. "Why, the blackguard … the rogue … the sneaky little … ugh! If he means to cut me out, I'll … I'll … ugh."

"Cut you out of what?" Alexander boomed.

"Out of the inheritance." She stepped out of the water, grabbed her wrapper and began pacing as she thrust her arms into the sleeves. Alexander could have sworn he heard Elliot sigh. "He told me he would go and see Miss Bromwell, to smooth things over after his pathetic display in Lady Westbury's garden. I assumed it had gone well, and he'd stayed for dinner. Why, the little weasel."

Alexander's blood raged through his veins. He wanted to grab her, shake the life from her, punish her for the part she'd played in this dastardly charade.

"There is no inheritance," he said, his words full of contempt. "You have made a mistake."

She stopped pacing and turned to face him, a frown marring her brow. "But that's impossible. Mr. Smythe said she was to inherit the sum of five thousand upon marriage, plus a monthly allowance from her father's estate."

"Mr. Smythe?" Elliot asked.

"The solicitor we … Henry paid for access to the files. He said her father was a wealthy plantation owner and sugar merchant."

While Alexander struggled to keep his hands at his sides, Elliot burst into fits of laughter.

"I hardly think this is the time for joviality," Alexander said. Murder was the only thought on his mind.

It took Elliot a moment to catch his breath. "I don't believe it," he said, putting his hand to his chest before dabbing at the corners of his eyes. "The lady you're talking about is Miss Bordwell."

Miss Sutherby looked aghast. "Miss Bordwell? You mean the dumpling of a girl with the turned-up nose?"

Elliot sucked in a breath. "Someone must have … must have made an error at the solicitor's office."

Miss Sutherby turned to Alexander. "You mean Miss Bromwell is not an heiress?"

"No, she's not. Now tell me where the hell Sutherby has taken her so I can wring his blasted neck."

"So that means Henry is going to marry Miss Bromwell for nothing." Miss Sutherby looked delighted and even clapped her hands. "Serves the devil right."

"Tell me where the hell she is!" Alexander shouted so loud, soot fluttered down the chimney and landed in the grate. He was tired of waiting, tired of listening. Fear clawed away at his heart, and his head felt thick and heavy.

Elliot stood and stepped forward. "My guess is they're on their way to Scotland. It is the only logical course of action. Sutherby believes he needs to marry her to get his hands on the money. He must have hired the carriage to take them north and across the border."

Alexander agreed with his assessment. Sutherby's only motivation was money, and he was convinced Evelyn was an heiress. But even if Sutherby was foolish enough to stop at a coaching inn, they'd never catch up with him. Not when their journey would be encumbered by the daylight hours.

A feeling of despair settled around him.

"We're just wasting time here," he said. "Let's—"

"Perhaps you're mistaken. Henry hasn't got the money to hire a carriage," Miss Sutherby interjected. "I'd managed to put some money away, but he didn't know—"

She stopped abruptly and rushed over to the bed. Using her back, she pushed the frame a few inches and scratched away at the floorboard.

"No!" she cried, opening the small wooden box and finding it empty. With a mournful wail, she tipped it upside down and shook it violently. "I'll kill him."

"Perhaps we should take her with us?" Elliot said, jerking his head towards the hunched figure on the floor. "We can't hand her over to the authorities. There's no evidence she's committed a crime, and it would only serve to embarrass Miss Bromwell."

Upon hearing their conversation, she shot to her feet and rushed to Elliot's side. "Take me with you. I could help you find him. I could act as a decoy. Then I'll string him up by his fancy cravat and leave him for the crows."

We may need to drink from her.

Elliot's words echoed through his mind. He'd rather die than submit to his depravity. He'd made a pact with himself never to drink directly from the source.

Never!

"Take me with you," she reiterated.

Alexander considered the request. It had taken a tremendous amount of effort to curb his temper. In a state of ravenous hunger, it would be nigh on impossible. Besides, to assist Miss Sutherby in any way would feel like a betrayal.

"We'll leave her here," he said firmly. He turned to Miss Sutherby, his tone revealing the anger brimming inside. "If you've got any sense, you'll pack your things and be gone by the time we return. If I set eyes on you again, I will not be responsible for my actions. These may be the clothes of a gentleman, but beneath them you'll find a monster."

Miss Sutherby put her hand to her mouth and stepped back, her eyes flashing with fear.

Alexander turned and strode to the door. "Come, we should be on our way."

Once outside, Elliot grabbed his arm. "You'll not be able to follow on horseback. It's too far, the risk too great. My carriage is equipped for such eventualities. We won't need to stop come dawn."

It was as though giant hands were squeezing all the air out of his lungs. An image of a golden-haired woman with devil hands flooded his mind. "You … you want me to ride in your carriage?"

"There is no other way."

CHAPTER 22

*T*he familiar sight of Mytton Grange brought memories of Alexander flooding back. That night when he'd stumbled upon her swimming in the river, when the touch of his hand had sent a rush of longing through her body, she'd felt a soul-deep connection that went beyond anything she had ever felt before.

Evelyn knew he could hear her thoughts. Perhaps it was a form of intuition. Perhaps their joining had strengthened the connection which was why she'd spent the whole journey calling out to him.

He would hear her silent plea. She was convinced of it. And so she closed her eyes and conjured a vivid image of her surroundings, infused it with love and passion.

"I never thought we'd get here," Mr. Sutherby said, disturbing her vision. "This windy weather is playing havoc with the roads. It has been the same for more than a week."

He spoke in his usual affable manner as though they were a married couple returning home after a long and arduous journey. The illusion was instantly shattered when she glanced down to see the hunting knife in his lap.

He picked up the length of rope at his side, twisting and wrapping it around into a loop before reaching across the carriage to grab her wrist. Evelyn fought him, kicked and struggled. The act was a way of showing her defiance even though she knew her efforts were in vain. She darted for the door, but the cold metal at her throat forced her back into her seat.

"Don't be like that," he said, his eyes all soft and angelic as he lowered the blade. "I want you to be happy. I want to see the smile that always warms my heart, the kindness that made me love you."

He dared to speak of love. After all he'd put her through, the man was quite clearly deranged.

"Then let me go. Let me ride back to London, and we need never mention it again." Her words carried an element of urgency, rang of desperation.

Sutherby gave a pitying smile, the sort given to sick children and injured animals. "You know I cannot do that. But when we are married—"

"While there's still breath in my body, that will never happen."

"You will change your mind when you see what I have planned for the evening."

The evening?

Evelyn glanced out of the carriage window. The sun was making its morning ascent. She had a whole day to escape from this lunatic. Stony Cross was but a few miles away. She would find her way there and wait for Alexander to come.

With the knife in his hand, he threw the rope into her lap. "Thread your hand through the loop."

Evelyn shook her head. "Why?"

"I thought we could go for a stroll around the grounds. Talk of our plans. But it would only spoil the moment if you were to run away."

"Do you think this is any way to treat the woman you wish to marry?"

Sutherby snorted. "I have done everything you've ever asked of me ... been polite, cordial. I have looked upon you like a delicate flower ... rare and precious. Yet you snub me in preference for your rude and arrogant friend, the Earl of Hale."

At the mere mention of his name her heart skipped a beat. "That is love, sir. It cannot be manipulated. It is not blind to one's faults. Love sees the truth in everything." She took a deep breath and found the courage to continue. "Your protestations are feigned. Your charity is born of selfishness, and as such you do not have the capacity to love."

Unperturbed by her words, he said. "But you will teach me. You will show me what I need to do to be a good husband. I am tired of wandering this world aimlessly. I need to settle with someone kind and good-natured."

"But I will never love you."

Sutherby shrugged. "What is love but folly?" He grabbed her wrist and pushed her hand through the loop, pulling it hard until the braided strands dug into her skin. "Come, there is nothing finer than a morning stroll to enliven the spirit."

They strolled around the garden, him pulling on the rope as if she were a disobedient dog that refused to keep up. He'd have to release her at some point, and she would bide her time until presented with an opportunity to escape.

"This would be a marvellous place to raise a family," Sutherby said, looking out across the vast expanse of patchwork fields.

Evelyn preferred the view to the south, the thick blanket of trees so dark and welcoming. She closed her eyes and inhaled deeply, imagining the scent of damp earth and pine. She recalled the night she trailed through the forest after Alexander, his lantern lighting the way. He'd been cold and distant. Nothing like the man she'd given herself to under the cherry tree.

Mr. Sutherby tugged the rope, forcing her to open her eyes and follow. "I believe children should be raised in the countryside, not amongst the filth and grime of the city," he said, leading her back towards the house.

"I don't want children." Her words were blunt to drive home the point that she was not a willing partner in this ridiculous charade.

"You will change your mind."

The coachman was engaged in tending to the horses. Luckily, there was hay in the stables, and he'd managed to pump clean water. Making their way in through the kitchen, Sutherby rooted around in cupboards and baskets but found nothing.

"That blasted housekeeper has cleaned the place out. There's not even a jar of preserves. I bet her family's supping like lords."

On the journey, the coachman had procured a meat pie and ale, but that had been hours ago. Her stomach rumbled at the prospect of a whole day and night without food.

"I'll send the coachman out," he continued. "The man will surely be able to find us something to eat." He sighed and pushed his hand through the mop of golden hair. "Come, there are things I must attend to, letters to write, plans for our departure."

"Departure? But I thought we were staying here."

Sutherby jerked his head back. "Only for this evening. If Hale comes looking for you, he'll follow the road north. We'll wait until tomorrow before setting out for Scotland."

Evelyn gulped. The man truly was insane.

He lifted his bare hand to stroke her cheek, and she turned her head in disgust.

"I've decided this will be our family home," he said,

grabbing her chin and forcing her to look at him. "We will consummate our alliance here this evening. You will have no option but to marry me then." He lowered his hand and placed his palm over her stomach. "Surely you would not wish our child to be born out of wedlock?"

"Our child! Have you gone completely mad?"

Catching him off guard, Evelyn tugged at the slackened rope in his hand and made a dart for the door. Before she could catch her breath, Sutherby was behind her. He swung her around, pulled her to his chest and kissed her roughly on the mouth.

"Do not mistake my kind overtures," he said, breaking contact. "I shall spill my seed inside you before the night is out. Whether you wish it so or not."

Without giving so much as a frown, he pulled her up the stairs and into the master chamber. Looping the rope around the bedpost, he secured it tightly, giving her no option but to sit on the bed. Taking another piece of rope, he grabbed her wrist and tied her other hand to the opposite post.

"I'll be back soon, my love," he said, offering a friendly smile full of warmth and kindness. "And then I shall make you mine."

"I'm telling you we've come too far. We're heading in the wrong direction." Alexander folded his arms across his chest and leant back against the carriage door. The feel of the cool night breeze upon his face brought a welcome relief from the oppressive confines of Elliot's conveyance.

"It won't hurt to check," Elliot said, banging on the door of the coaching inn.

"We need to turn around."

They'd only come as far as Barnet. With every stage of

the twelve-mile journey, he'd felt his connection to Evelyn weaken. Now, the invisible threads were strained to the point he feared they might snap.

Alexander had not set foot inside a carriage for two years, let alone take a long journey in one. During the first few miles, he had struggled to breathe. The lack of air to his lungs made it too difficult to think. When the faint images of Stony Cross first penetrated his addled mind, interspersed with pictures of a brooding castle and the Devil's disciple, he dismissed them. But the forest in Bavaria was soon overshadowed by the forest in Hampshire. The mouth of Satan was replaced by the soft, sweet lips of an angel.

"No one fitting their description has passed through," Elliot said, coming to stand before him. "I'd have known if he was lying."

Alexander straightened. "We need to go to Hampshire."

Elliot glanced up at the night sky. "But it's a twelve-hour journey, not including the two hours we've wasted travelling here or time to rest the horses."

"She's in Hampshire. I sense it."

"If we turn back, and they're on their way to Scotland, you'll never catch up with them."

"I know. But something feels wrong. I need to go back."

"You're certain this is the course you wish to take?"

Alexander fell silent, mindful of the strange sensation in his chest whenever he thought of Evelyn. Somehow, their souls were connected. He had to trust in the power of whatever wonderful spell Fate had woven. He had to trust his instincts.

"She's in Hampshire. I know it."

Elliot sighed. "Very well. Hampshire it is." His expression darkened. "We'll not get there until dusk. Sutherby's been alone with her for—"

"You do not need to remind me," he said through gritted teeth.

Elliot held his hands up. "I just think you need to be prepared. There's no telling what situation we may find."

Alexander stepped forward, his gaze hard and unforgiving. "If he's harmed her in any way, I'm going to kill him. I'm going to drain every drop of blood from his pathetic little body until there's nothing left but a limp, withered shell."

"I understand your need for vengeance, my friend. But I won't let you. I won't let you become the monster you've spent so long trying to avoid. Why do you think I went back for provisions?"

"Perhaps it's time I stopped hiding. Perhaps it's time I accepted who I really am."

"And what will you tell Miss Bromwell?"

"The truth."

She deserved nothing less. He should never have left it so long.

Elliot gripped his shoulder. "Whatever has happened in the past, you're a good man, Alexander. Always remember that."

The apprehension in Elliot's tone caused doubt to flare, but he brushed it aside.

Elliot issued instructions to his coachman. As they settled into their seats, Elliot pulled the stopper from the bottle of blood and swigged the contents.

"What does it feel like?" Elliot said, his gaze curious as he lounged back against the plush squab. "What does it feel like to love another with all your heart?"

How could one define something so perfect, something so profound?

Alexander smiled. "It feels like heaven."

CHAPTER 23

*E*velyn was lying on the bed, her hands still tied to the posts, when Mr. Sutherby entered. She shot up and scrambled back, her feet slipping against the coverlet in her haste to reach the headboard.

"Here we are." He put the tray on the end of the bed. "Thankfully, Briggs managed to find a few provisions in the village, enough to tide us over until tomorrow. I'll just nip and get the wine."

She stared at the silver tray. The decorative plates contained a varied assortment: slices of salt beef, cheese, scotch eggs and pickles. The cutlery was tarnished, and there were a few wilting tulips presented in a crystal bud vase.

Mr. Sutherby returned, minus his coat, with a pitcher of wine and two glasses and placed them on the dressing table. When he raised his hand to pour, she noticed the hunting knife, sheathed and tucked into the band of his breeches.

"What time is it?" she asked, glancing at the window. The sky's orange-brown glow heralded the onset of dusk. Had Alexander heard her plea? As the daylight faded, so did all hope.

"It's almost eight." Mr. Sutherby walked over to the bed and untied one hand. He rubbed the grazed skin at her wrist before bringing her a glass of wine, to which she turned up her nose. "Drink it. It will make the evening much more pleasant, make you feel more congenial."

Congenial to what? She'd need a hundred barrels to ease her anxiety. Perhaps if she showed willing, he might untie the other rope, and so she took the wine whilst offering a feigned smile.

Mr. Sutherby proceeded to light a few candles before drawing the drapes. "Forgive me," he said, joining her on the bed, and her racing heart settled when he began distributing the food between two plates. "I've left you alone for far too long, but I wanted to give you time to rest. I wanted to give you time to become accustomed to the idea of a lifelong partnership."

"A gentleman would have been more attentive," she said, trying to keep her tone even when all she wanted to do was rant and curse. "A gentleman would not hurt a lady in such a vile and despicable manner."

He glanced at the rope and looked genuinely sorry. "When we are wed, I shall make amends. When you're mine, I shall devote my life to your happiness. And you will soon see this as a necessary step to secure our future."

She handed him the wine glass, took the plate he offered with an eager hand, her grumbling stomach feeling no prejudice. Having spent the whole day alone in the room, she'd been so ravenous she'd have eaten the bed sheets. And so she grabbed a piece of beef and tore at it like a fox would a rabbit.

Mr. Sutherby stared at her, and she froze mid-mouthful.

"You see," he said, offering a smile. "You feel more comfortable with me already. You'll be pleased to hear I have had a rather productive day. I have written to your aunt—"

"My aunt?" Poor Aunt Bea would be worried beyond measure. "What have you said to her?"

"I've explained our need to elope and ask she waits for our return before announcing the wonderful news."

What in blazes was wrong with him? Either he was too simple to appreciate the gravity of his actions or was too cunning to care.

"And what need forces us to take such drastic action?" she said, anger rising to the surface.

"As your aunt heartily approves of our match, there is only one reason why a couple would elope." Mr. Sutherby placed their plates back on the tray. "Don't get upset. I'll be as gentle as I can. When you're used to it, it can be a very pleasurable experience." His beady gaze drifted up the length of her leg and he moistened his lips. "Perhaps we should dispense with all of this and just get on with—"

"You'll leave me the hell alone."

"I had hoped the meal and conversation would settle your nerves, but I can sense your apprehension and fear." He stood and moved the tray to the floor. "It is to be expected. The process will be easier if you relax a little."

Relax! Evelyn felt nauseous at the thought of him touching her. She'd fight him until her last breath.

Picking up the piece of rope still attached to the post, he grabbed her wrist, holding it between both hands before securing it tightly.

"Leave me the hell alone," she cried, the tugging action only causing the rope to burn into the raw skin.

Mr. Sutherby stood back with his hands on his hips as he surveyed her clothing. "It would be easier if you were undressed as I detest the fumbling about. But I've waited long enough. Besides, it will appease your need for modesty, and I shall just have to use my imagination."

He placed the knife on the dressing table. She kicked

him as he crawled up onto the bed and he grabbed her ankles and sat on them while he unbuttoned the fall of his breeches.

"It will be over quite quickly, I fear."

"Get off me! I'll never marry you." She writhed back and forth but felt his cold hands slide up her thighs, the icy chill freezing her blood. "Get your damn hands off me."

"Once I breach your maidenhead," he panted, pressing down on top of her until she could hardly breathe, "we will be eternally joined."

"You're too late," she cried, the words accompanied by a sinister chuckle. "I have already given myself to another."

Mr. Sutherby froze but then snorted. "Your lies don't fool me. Nothing you can say will stop me taking you tonight."

"No," a deep masculine voice roared, "but I bloody well will."

Suddenly the room appeared brighter, and she could breathe again. When she looked up, the first thing she saw was Mr. Sutherby's feet dangling in the air, his legs jerking back and forth like a *marionette*. Then she heard the loud thud as Alexander threw him to the floor.

Alexander.

Her heart fluttered in her chest, relief causing her to sigh.

Oblivious to Mr. Sutherby's cries of protest, she stared as Alexander delivered a heavy blow to the man's stomach. For good measure, he punched Sutherby on the nose, the blood spurting instantly.

"Alexander. You came."

Leaving Mr. Sutherby in a crumpled heap, he rushed to her side and sat down on the edge of the bed. "Has he hurt you?" he said, cupping her face and kissing her softly on the mouth.

Evelyn shook her head. "No. I'm fine." She stared into his silver-blue eyes, the rush of love and longing taking her breath away. "You came," she repeated softly. "You came just in time."

"I'd have been here sooner but—"

"I know. The wind has caused no end of trouble on the roads."

With deft fingers, he untied the ropes binding her to the bed. When he saw the pinky-red welts branded into her skin, he cursed. "I may yet kill him for what he's done to you."

"It doesn't matter. They'll heal. All that matters is you're here."

She could feel the anger emanating from him, the vibration wild and erratic.

"It took every ounce of strength I possess not to rip his throat out," he said, bringing her wrist to his lips and raining featherlight kisses along the grooved sores.

"It would only serve to cause an even greater scandal."

His expression grew dark. "About Sutherby. He … he thinks you're an heiress."

"An heiress? Why would he think that?"

"There was some confusion at the solicitor's office. He was told you'd inherit five thousand pounds upon marriage." Alexander shook his head. "I'm sorry."

"There's nothing to be sorry about. I always knew he was hiding something. He was always far too affable. It's not as though it's a great shock to discover he was only interested in money."

"There's something else," he said, a little hesitant. "Charlotte Sutherby is not his sister. She's his accomplice, his lover, although she had no idea that he'd kidnapped you. Greed prevailed over loyalty, and he was reluctant to share the money."

Evelyn gasped, although nothing shocked or surprised her after the trauma of recent events. "No wonder she was so keen to see us wed. Goodness, is there anything else you need to tell me?"

Alexander's face turned ashen, and his gaze fell to his lap.

There was something else.

She'd only said the words in jest. But of course, he was referring to the reason he'd locked himself away, to the terrible scandal she didn't give a hoot about.

His expression turned grave. "Eve … I … there is something you need to know. Something about me."

He looked so terrified she felt nauseous.

"No!" The word came out as a shriek, and she was suddenly overcome with a strange sense of foreboding. No, stronger than that … more akin to dread, to panic. "Don't tell me. I do not need to know. Let us leave it in the past. Let us leave here, forget everything that has happened before this moment and never speak of it again."

"We can't."

"It doesn't matter."

"It matters a great deal."

She heard anguish, a deep sense of sorrow and her heart was beating so loudly she feared her chest could not contain it. Perhaps fear had clouded her vision for she failed to notice Mr. Sutherby lunging at the bed.

"You'll not take her," Sutherby yelled, slashing at Alexander's arm and face with his knife. The material of Alexander's coat took the brunt of the damage, yet she noticed the thin line of blood across his cheek.

With a loud roar, Alexander flew off the bed, knocking the knife to the floor.

Mr. Sutherby shuffled back, his eyes large and wild, his bottom lip quivering. "No … no … don't touch me. Don't hurt me," he muttered, but Alexander grabbed him and sank his teeth deep into his neck.

Evelyn screamed as Sutherby's eyes rolled back in their sockets, as he gasped and heaved in sheer terror.

The door to the chamber burst open, and Lord Markham rushed in, stopping dead in his tracks. "Bloody hell." He raced over to Alexander. "That's enough," he bellowed. "Leave him, Alexander. Leave him be."

Alexander ignored his plea.

She could see trails of blood trickling down Mr. Sutherby's yellow waistcoat.

Lord Markham grabbed Alexander's arm. "Don't do this. You're scaring Miss Bromwell."

Evelyn scrambled off the bed. If he killed Mr. Sutherby, their lives would be forever tainted by such an evil deed. "Please, Alexander. Let him go."

The sound of her voice seemed to have some effect. He released Sutherby, the man collapsing to the floor, limp and lifeless. Lord Markham bent down and examined the wound, licking his fingers and dabbing at the holes in Sutherby's neck.

Nothing could have prepared her for the terrifying sight that greeted her when Alexander turned around.

His beautiful blue eyes were a lifeless black, the rest a mass of scrawny red veins. Blood dripped from the points of two sharp fangs, running down his lips and chin, staining the collar of his white shirt. His breathing sounded wild, hoarse, a dreadful hissing.

She shrank back from him in horror.

"What … what are you?" Her voice was barely a whisper. She gulped down a breath to stop a sob from escaping.

He took a step towards her. She backed away, her legs and arms shaking so violently she felt dizzy. She rubbed her wrists, the stinging pain proof that the devilish vision before her was real and not some figment of her overwrought imagination.

"Eve. Let me explain."

His voice sounded strange, far too deep, foreign to her ears. "Stay … stay back. Stay away from me," she stuttered, her hands held out in front of her as she backed out of the chamber door.

He blinked rapidly, and she saw faint flickers of blue streaking through his eyes. The blackness passed quickly, and he appeared more like himself. Yet he was changed in her eyes. The man she knew and loved was now lost to her, relegated to a pile of distant memories.

The pain in her chest grew more intense, choking as it rose up to her throat and her only thought was to run, to run far away from the evil nightmare. Turning on her heels, she raced out into the hall and down the stairs, checking over her shoulder in case he followed her. Relief coursed through her as she ran out into the cool night air.

But she didn't stop—she couldn't stop.

The need to be free from the ache in her heart was overwhelming, and she kept running, across the dew-soaked grass, through clusters of shrubs and trees—for half a mile or more. When her legs could no longer support her weight, she collapsed in a heap on the forest floor. The world around her was as dark and as black as her soul, and she sobbed until the tears stung her skin.

"Why!" The mournful cry echoed through the forest, and she glanced up at the thick canopy, hoping to find a ray of light.

Wrapping her arms around her stomach, she rocked back and forth in a bid to calm her breathing. The grief was immeasurable. A vast hole had opened in her chest. She felt so cold, so utterly alone.

"Alexander," she whispered. "I love you."

But the words brought with it fresh tears aplenty. She understood it all now. His need to hide away. His reluctance to commit. If only he were debt-ridden. She would have lived with him in poverty. She would have done anything.

I can't be the man you want me to be.

The words shot straight to her heart like a barbed arrow, ripping into the weak, flimsy flesh.

Love was unconditional—she'd told herself that many times. Love was not blind to one's faults and imperfections. Love accepted them as part of the complicated whole. She'd said as much to Mr. Sutherby. But this … this was …

What was this strange affliction that would see a man become a monster?

I don't want to hurt you?

Those words made sense now. He would never hurt her; she knew that. Perhaps the essence of the man still existed deep inside the abhorrent form. Despite his monstrous countenance, she recalled catching a hint of sorrow in his dark eyes; she recalled a hint of self-loathing.

Guilt tore at her heart.

He had tried to tell her, tried to explain. But she'd refused to listen.

All the promises she'd made. All the love she'd professed —now she couldn't shake the feeling that she had let him down. She had turned her back on him when he had needed her most. But she'd been so scared.

"Miss Bromwell."

The gentle voice penetrated the madness. She looked up to see the dark figure of Lord Markham standing over her.

"Come," he said softly, offering his hand. "Let me see you safely to the inn. Let me help you. Let me help you forget your pain."

CHAPTER 24

*L*ord Markham hired the private parlour at the inn, the room being small with a low ceiling and thick timber beams supporting its five-hundred-year-old history. Evelyn settled into the chair by the fire, the heat doing nothing to ease her trembling limbs as she cupped her hands around the goblet and sipped the wine.

"Don't worry," Lord Markham said, nodding to the pewter vessel. "I watched him wipe it clean with a napkin. Would you like me to call for a blanket?"

"No. I'll be fine. I'll soon warm up."

A knock on the door brought a serving wench who plonked an earthenware flagon and mug on the table. She gave the lord a cheeky grin to suggest she had more to offer than refreshments.

"You don't need to stay," Evelyn said, aware of his wandering gaze following the sway of the woman's hips as she left the room.

"I cannot leave you here alone. Apparently, I'm to try a mug of cider. Mr. Harlow was adamant. It's the best I'll find for miles around."

Evelyn forced a weak smile before turning to stare at the golden flames dancing in the hearth.

She had lost everything tonight.

All her hopes and dreams had been ripped from her fingers. Now, a feeling of utter hopelessness consumed her, shrouded her in grief and misery. She glanced at Lord Markham, who still appeared unperturbed by the horrifying events of the evening.

"When you saw him, when you saw Alexander's strange countenance, you were not shocked or afraid," she said, trying to find the courage to talk about the devastating moment when her whole world changed.

"No," Markham replied, his expression turning solemn. "It is nothing new to me."

"You have witnessed it before?"

Markham shuffled in his seat and gazed into the fire. "In a manner of speaking."

The terrifying image came flooding back: the blood-soaked fangs, the devilish eyes. "No matter how hard I try I cannot make sense of it. It defies all reason and logic."

"There are many things in this world that cannot be explained," he replied cryptically.

"But I watched him change before my eyes. How can that be?"

Lord Markham stood and walked over to the table, pulled the stopper from the flagon and filled the mug. He took a large swig and winced. "Good heavens, I've never tasted anything so sour. No wonder the landlord is trying to get rid of the stuff."

"No doubt he saw your fine clothes and charged you double. But you're avoiding my question, my lord."

The corners of his mouth curved up. "What do you want to know?"

"Everything."

"The story is not fit for the ears of an innocent lady."

Innocent? She'd given her virginity to her lover. She'd been kidnapped by a madman, was now sitting in a private room with an unmarried gentleman. Her reputation was beyond saving. Indeed, her broken heart cared for nothing but easing the pain.

Lifting her chin, she said, "Perhaps I am not as innocent as you would believe."

His gaze drifted over her. "Perhaps. But why should I tell you?"

Because she wanted to understand what had happened to Alexander. Her heart still ached for him. "Because I love him. I think I deserve an explanation."

"Ah, love. Is it not just a fairy tale for the weak-minded?" He went to take another swig of cider but changed his mind and placed the mug on the table. "I think the events of the evening have proved that love is nothing but torture and pain."

"That's not true," she said, drawing on the love she felt for Alexander. She recalled the way his touch ignited her soul, the way his words eased her fears, the way his body took her beyond this mundane world to a distant magical plane. "Love cannot be defined. It is God's greatest gift. Sustenance for the soul. Love is caring for another so deeply—"

"Caring?" Lord Markham scoffed. "Where is your love now, Miss Bromwell? I shall tell you. He is wallowing in his grief, lost to the night that has claimed him as his own. He is hurting, and he is alone. Forsaken."

The blunt words caused her tears to fall.

She imagined Alexander sitting on the bench by the fountain, weeds curling up around his boots, a ghostly mist clawing at his shoulders. In her vision, he looked so sad and tortured as he begged for the Lord to release him from the Devil's curse.

Pain turned to anger and resentment. "Do you think I want it to be this way?" she cried, jumping to her feet. "Do you think my heart is not crying out in pain?"

They stared at each other for a moment before Lord Markham bowed his head and said, "Sit. Sit down and I will tell you."

Evelyn flopped down into the chair and tried to calm her ragged breathing. "Help me to understand, my lord. That is all I ask of you."

Lord Markham sat opposite her, stretched out his legs and crossed them at the ankles. "There is a woman in Bavaria. A woman beautiful enough to send a thousand legions into battle to fight for the right to possess her. But her heart is tainted, her body plagued by a demon. One bite from such a woman brings about a devastating change that can never be undone."

Evelyn sat forward. "Are you saying Alexander received such a bite?"

Was this the terrible event Alexander referred to?

"Not just Alexander. There are a few of us."

Us!

Evelyn tried to swallow down the solid lump in her throat. She scanned the gentleman before her, aware that her eyes had grown wide. "You mean you are one of these creatures? You have also been a recipient?"

Lord Markham smiled. "Yes, Miss Bromwell. I do not fear Alexander because I understand his torment ... because I suffer from the same horrifying affliction."

Her heart missed a beat.

"So, you are able to make your eyes turn black?" she said, digging her nails into the wooden arms of the chair. "You're able to grow teeth sharp enough to kill a man?"

"I am." He nodded. "But there is more to it than that. We cannot go out in the daylight. Our skin is too sensitive to the sun. We cannot eat and drink as you do, but must supplement our diet with blood."

"Blood!" She shot out of the chair.

"Calm yourself. We drink animal blood. I am not about to sink my teeth into your vein and drain the life from you."

Evelyn's hand flew up to her throat. "I—I should hope not. Have you ever … ever—"

"Killed anyone? No. We may look abhorrent when we feed naturally, but we are not savages, Miss Bromwell. Sutherby caught Alexander off guard that is all. His need to protect you drove him to act as he did."

When Alexander had sat on the bed, she had sensed the rage burning within. But he'd kept it at bay, showed only concern for her, kept his voice soft and tender.

"Mr. Sutherby provoked him," she said, wishing she could throttle the man for his interference. "He attacked Alexander with a knife."

"Uncontrollable anger is often a trigger. It is the point where animal instinct overtakes rational thought."

Evelyn considered his words. She would probably fly into an uncontrollable rage if she'd been slashed with a blade. Discussing things so openly made it all seem less terrifying, and she owed Lord Markham a debt of gratitude. "You are a good and loyal friend, my lord."

He scoffed. "Such a good friend, I have left him alone in his greatest hour of need."

The thought of Alexander all lost and alone caused guilt to flare.

"Then you must go to him," she said, walking over to Lord Markham and placing her hand on his sleeve. The gentleman stared at her fingers as he sucked in a breath. "He needs you more than I."

"I cannot leave you here alone. Heaven knows what sort of characters hover in the shadows."

"Pay the wench to sit with me, just for a few hours while you attend to Alexander. The only thing I ask is that you assist me in returning to London."

His gaze turned sharp and curious as he rose from the chair. "I have the ability to make you forget. I could make you forget what you saw." He sighed. "But then Alexander would always know the truth of it, and I doubt he would embrace you as before."

Her mouth felt dry, her heart palpitating in her throat. Lord Markham was right. Alexander would always know she had broken her promise. He would always know her love came with certain conditions, and it would never be the same as before.

"There is another answer to your dilemma," Lord Markham continued. "I could make you forget you ever met him. He would be a stranger to you. It is what he has asked me to do."

Alexander wanted her to forget him?

It was as though someone had reached down into her soul and ripped it right out. He could make her forget everything. There would be no memory of Alexander stripping naked for his swim, of the way she had reacted to the magnificent sight. There would be no memory of the beautiful sketch, of their glorious kiss in the orangery.

She'd forget the feel of his body when he moved inside her.

She'd forget what it felt like to love him.

"No." Her word was barely more than a whisper. "No. Promise me you won't do it. I don't want to forget. I don't want to forget any of it."

Lord Markham exhaled. "I shall make the arrangements with Mr. Harlow. I shall ask that his wife sit with you in here until I return. You will lock the door and not permit anyone else to enter. Is that understood?"

Evelyn nodded.

"When I return, we will leave immediately for London." He pulled out his watch and examined it beneath the candle-light. "You must understand, the nature of our circumstance cannot become public knowledge. I will speak to Alexander, but ultimately I must do what I feel is appropriate."

"I would not breathe a word of it to anyone. You must trust me in that."

Lord Markham had the look of a man who trusted no one.

"Give me two hours," he said, moving to the door. "And lock this behind me."

Mrs. Harlow was a short, stout woman with ruddy cheeks, and hands so dry and chapped they left a dusting of flaky skin on her brown dress.

"Your brother is mighty worried about you," she said, settling down in the chair by the fire. She folded her arms across her chest to support her drooping bosom and appeared grateful for the opportunity to take a much-needed rest. No doubt Lord Markham had paid handsomely for the pleasure.

"My brother," Evelyn said, trying not to smile. "Yes, he is most attentive."

"It always comes down to family in the end. We all need someone to offer support and guidance. More so, when you're just getting ready to fledge the nest."

Oh, she'd taken that first leap; she'd fluttered her wings and soared through the air, carried on a breeze of resplendent pleasure. Only, she was not as strong as she'd thought and had come crashing back down to reality.

Mrs. Harlow was right. Everyone needed support at some

time. Aunt Beatrice had been there for her when her parents had died, and she couldn't imagine what it would have been like to be alone.

Alexander had suffered, too. Only he'd had no one to turn to. And so he had shut himself away from the world and barred the door to all visitors.

After her bitter betrayal, she doubted he would ever smile again. And he looked so handsome with laughter flashing in his eyes. The thought brought to mind his reaction to her tipping pond water over her head, to the way his eyes twinkled as he picked algae from her hair.

Another wonderful memory that would crumble to dust if Lord Markham wished it so.

"Never mind, miss," Mrs. Harlow said, mistaking her forlorn expression. "You'll soon be on your way home. Your brother said you'll be leaving for London this very night."

Soon she'd be in London and then thousands of miles away in India. Poor Aunt Bea must be so worried. Her thoughts turned to the man responsible for causing her misery. She'd not even thought to ask what had happened to Mr. Sutherby.

"Some ladies don't like to travel in the dark," Mrs. Harlow continued, "not through the forest."

"Oh, I don't mind the dark. I find it peaceful, magical almost. I always struggle to settle at night. If I had my way, I would sleep away the day."

Mrs. Harlow narrowed her gaze. "Well, all folks are different, I suppose."

The night is my home. It is where I belong.

Alexander's words flooded her mind. The night was where she belonged, too. But she had let him down. He would never forgive her, never trust her again.

Perhaps she could try—try to understand him, to help him, to love him.

Hope blossomed in her chest.

Any life without him was not a life worth living. She had to be with him. She would give up her days to slumber, spend her nights in his company.

She would give up everything for him.

A tap on the door disturbed her dreams and Mrs. Harlow eased out of the chair and answered it. Evelyn heard her muttered protests and groans of discontent.

"I'll be but a few minutes," she said, already halfway out of the door. "Someone's asking for a hot supper, and I swear that girl's never set foot in a kitchen her entire life. Now lock this door behind me."

As Evelyn turned the key, she was suddenly hit with a deep pang of sorrow, a heart-wrenching sense of anguish. It wasn't her own pain she was feeling.

Eve.

The word resonated like an ear-piercing cry. He needed her.

"Alexander," she whispered as she unlocked the door with trembling fingers. "I'm coming."

CHAPTER 25

"*Y*ou let Sutherby go!" Alexander thrust his arms behind his back for fear of lashing out. "What the hell were you thinking? The man deserves to swing for what he's done."

"Well, I didn't *just* let him go," Elliot said with a mischievous grin. He picked up the glass from the side table and sipped the blood. "I used a little mind magic. He's probably wandering the woods looking for fairies. I convinced him his life depended upon rescuing a hundred and he's only got a week to achieve the task."

Alexander paced back and forth in front of the fire. Being back at Stony Cross reminded him of Eve. Her presence lingered in the hallways, in his parlour, in his study. When he'd ventured into the garden, his mind conjured her image watching him from the upstairs window, and he called out her name in his grief.

"And you think that a fitting punishment for kidnap and whatever else he intended to do?"

"I was thinking of Miss Bromwell's precarious reputation," Elliot said with a hint of frustration. "She'll be ruined if word of this gets out. Besides, someone had to tend to Suther-by's wound. Someone had to ensure he remembered nothing of how he came by it."

Alexander brushed his hand through his hair. "And for that I'm grateful. I wasn't thinking clearly when I left you there with him. I didn't thank you for dealing with his coach-man." The only thing on his mind had been the look of sheer terror on Eve's face. He'd felt her fear like the slash of a sword, slicing through his stomach, his guts spilling out onto the floor.

It was his fault. He should have told her before. He should have controlled his urges.

"You were not thinking clearly *then*," Elliot said, draining his glass and slamming it down on the table, "and you're not thinking clearly now."

"What is that supposed to mean?"

"I know little of love." Elliot's dandified wave and curled lip conveyed disdain, as though the word was foreign to his repertoire. "But I know Miss Bromwell believes she loves you deeply. Yet still you would have her forget you. Are you certain there is no hope of helping her to understand? Can you not—"

"You saw her face," he said, picking up the poker and prodding the fire. "She despises what I am. To her, I will always be an abhorrence, a distortion of all that is normal and natural."

"Those are your words, not hers."

"They are true all the same. She could never love me as she used to."

He wished he could go back to the time when all he felt was anger and bitterness. He wished he had no knowledge of love's beautiful ache. Self-pity was not a quality he admired, yet he could not help but grieve for all he had lost.

He twirled the iron rod between his fingers and thrust the

handle at Elliot. "If you want to help, you can start by driving this through my heart, or what's left of it."

In a sudden fit of rage, Elliot seized the poker and shot to his feet knocking Alexander to the floor with a punch to his chest. "You want to bloody well die," he spat, "then let me put you out of your misery." The point of the poker dug deep into Alexander's skin, and Elliot put his boot on his chest to keep him on the floor.

"Do it," Alexander cried, his heart too weak to protest. "I have nothing left to live for."

"Know this," Elliot said, his face red and distorted in his rage. "Miss Bromwell does not want to forget you, and I will honour her wishes. Know that she will always remember the love you shared. Her nightmares will be haunted by the image of a monster. She will always know what you have forsaken, know that you're a coward."

Elliot's taunts failed to penetrate his shield of despair.

All except one.

"You promised me you would make her forget, that you would erase her pain."

"I did not promise you anything, Alexander. But know that in your absence, I will pursue Miss Bromwell. Perhaps I will take her to Bavaria and beg the golden-haired goddess to turn her."

"No!" The word sounded like a howl as he unleashed the wrath of the devil inside. He felt his fangs protract as his vision sharpened. Drawing all his strength, he writhed and kicked out as Elliot struggled to contain him.

Elliot threw the poker to the floor and stumbled back. "This is who you are. The sooner you learn to accept it, the easier your life will become."

"I should rip your throat out for your callous remarks."

"But you won't," Elliot said with a smirk.

Alexander stepped back, feeling disgust for the beastly

image he knew marred his face. "Just leave me the hell alone."

Stalking away without another word, he marched through the house and out into the garden. The fresh night air failed to bring the usual relief, and so he wandered over to the bench, flopped down and buried his head in his hands.

Now he knew all his efforts to occupy his mind during the long, lonely nights had been for naught. Nothing would fill those hours now. Whenever he sat at his easel, he would think of her. Whenever he glanced at the moon's reflection glistening upon the water, he would recall the night he'd watched an angel swim. The scent of cherry blossoms would remind him of the intoxicating taste of her skin, of the night she gave herself to him.

"Alexander."

Just to torture him all the more, his mind conjured the sweet sound of her voice. The soft timbre was more beautiful than any musical arrangement he'd ever heard, and he closed his eyes and tried to imagine it again.

"Please, Alexander. I know I've hurt you, but give me a chance to explain."

His eyes flew open as he felt a hand on his shoulder, the warmth rushing to his heart in a desperate bid to stoke the burnt debris.

"Eve." He shot up and swung around, forgetting his teeth still overhung his bottom lip, that his eyes were not the blue she remembered.

She gasped and swallowed visibly, her head jerking back in shock and he wanted to scream and curse. In his shame, he shuffled back, his gaze falling from her wide eyes.

"Don't hide from me," she suddenly said, rushing around the bench to stand in front of him. "Let me look upon your face."

"It is the face of a beast."

"No, Alexander. It is the face of the man I love." She put her hand on his chest, and his heart pounded against his ribs. "I love you, and I want you to know that I'm not afraid."

He struggled to believe her pretty protestations. His faith in all things just and equal having deserted him. Still, he longed to hold her close, to kiss away his fears.

Alexander raised his head, and her hand moved up to caress his cheek. Her fingers trembled against his skin, and he found he admired her all the more for her courage. Blinking back a torrent of emotion, he covered her hand.

Desire, love and longing pulsed through him.

Eve looked tenderly into his eyes. "Please say something. Say you forgive me."

He was suddenly overcome with the urge to release all his pent-up emotion.

"I … I love you," he said softly. "You are everything to me, which is why I want you to forget you ever met me. Let your life be free of this hideous burden."

He watched a tear trickle down her cheek and guilt flared.

"I have something to ask of you," she said, lifting her chin.

"Ask what you will. But know that I only desire your happiness."

"Good," she said, her voice sounding strong, more confident, "because I want you to marry me. I want you to be my husband, my lover, my friend and companion. Let me live here with you. We shall spend the nights together. During the days, you may sketch me whilst I sleep."

Marriage?

The sense of remorse that always accompanied unobtainable dreams burst through him. In his wild and vivid imagination, he could almost picture the blissful scene.

"There's more to this affliction than my strange countenance." His voice sounded more natural as his features returned to their human form. "Things beyond your comprehension."

She smiled up at him. "You don't like the sun, and you drink blood."

"Elliot told you?"

"He also told me about the golden-haired lady."

Alexander sucked in a breath. "She's no lady. But those things are not what trouble me most."

"Tell me. Tell me everything."

Unable to resist the urge clawing away inside, he took her face in his hands and caressed the soft skin. "What if I can't control the beast inside? What if you grow more frightened of me each day? I couldn't bear to see fear in your eyes."

"I'm not afraid anymore."

Alexander snorted, recalling the harrowing image of her fleeing through the chamber door in terror. "You may say that now, but what if the episodes become more frequent? In a year, things might be different."

She put her hands on his chest and all of his fears melted away. "What if you tire of me, Alexander?"

He pulled her into his arms and held her tight. "My love for you has no limits," he said, stroking her hair.

Eve looked up to gaze into his eyes. "I would rather spend every day loving you than spend a lifetime alone. And I *would* be alone, Alexander, for there will never be another. Not for me."

At some point in his life, he must have done something wonderful to deserve the love of an angel. Struggling to contain his raging emotions, he brushed his lips across hers, the brief touch causing their passion to flame.

"Let us make each night we spend together more precious than the last," he said, his voice brimming with desire as he surrendered to the light.

She stepped away from him, a coy smile playing on her lips. "Then let us begin right now, with a swim."

Alexander scanned her dress. "We'll need to be less encumbered."

They stripped off their clothes in great haste. He helped her with buttons and undergarments before throwing their discarded items on the bench.

Holding hands, they walked down to the river's edge; the moon's incandescence casting a silvery sheen over their bare skin. As Alexander helped her down into the water, swimming was the last thing on his mind. But the cold was biting, his desire momentarily overshadowed by the sharp shock and he pulled her into an embrace to ease her shivering limbs.

"We should move if we're to keep warm," he said as desire burst forth again with its usual intensity and he poured it all into a devilishly sinful kiss.

In the water, they were weightless, and she wrapped her legs around him with ease. "Don't wait," she whispered against his mouth, her thigh brushing against the only part of his anatomy impervious to the cold. "I want to join with you —now, tonight, forever."

"Your happiness is all I seek," he said, as he positioned himself and pushed inside her, giving her everything she needed. "I love you."

She threw her head back, her perfect breasts ripe for the offering, and he took her nipple into his mouth as he thrust deeper.

"I love you," she said between breathless pants.

As she cried his name in the wild throes of her pleasure, one thought pushed to the fore.

He was no longer a lost soul wandering the darkness.

He had found his way home.

EPILOGUE

"*I*t took a little mind manipulation," Alexander said, "but the bishop had no choice when faced with the wrath of an earl. He insisted that I call the next morning, although he soon understood that the evening suited me much better."

"And now she's your wife." Leo nodded over to Eve as she chatted with their guests. "You're a braver man than I."

Elliot patted him on the back. "You're definitely lucky. I doubt there's another woman alive who would choose to marry a man plagued with our afflictions. Your wife is a true original."

Alexander glanced at Eve with pride. Sensing his gaze, she looked up and smiled. "She'll always be unique in my eyes, but there's nothing original about love."

Leo shivered visibly. "Just hearing the word makes me want to run for the hills."

"Have no fear," Elliot said with a chuckle. "The day either of us declares love will be the day the sun fails to rise."

"I used to be just as cynical." Had Eve not thrown the stone through his window, he'd most likely still be brooding in his chair. "Nothing can prepare you for such a delicious form of agony."

Leo's eyes widened. "It's the agony that terrifies me. That constant pining I hear so much about."

"Trust me, your day will come, although I have a strange feeling Elliot will be the first to fall. And I shall look forward to the day with eager anticipation."

Elliot scoffed. "You'll be waiting an exceedingly long time, my friend."

Alexander sipped his brandy, but it still made the muscles in his throat spasm.

"If you drank it more often, you'd soon get used to it," Elliot said. "I'm assuming it was your idea to have an informal supper as opposed to a wedding breakfast."

"My wife thought it would save me having to explain why I'd not touched a morsel. I did nibble on a sandwich, but I spat it into the plant pot when no one was looking."

That wasn't quite true. Mrs. Shaw had witnessed the whole thing, but it seemed nothing could erase the smile she'd worn for days.

Leo's eyes bulged. "Who's that?" he said, nodding to a pretty lady with honey-gold hair. "She is trying to act all demure though I swear she keeps looking over here."

"That is Mr. Hartwood's niece, and she is strictly off bounds."

"This penchant for golden hair worries me," Elliot said. "If I'm not mistaken, I'd say you have unresolved issues from your traumatic experience in Bavaria."

Leo screwed up his nose. "Don't be so ridiculous. I have no preference when it comes to women. I'll take them any way I find them."

"Prove it," Elliot said with an arrogant grin. "I'll wager twenty pounds you end up bedding a golden-haired goddess at the masquerade tomorrow night."

Leo thrust his hand out though there was a flicker of uncertainty in his eyes. "Done."

Alexander chuckled. Perhaps there was no hope of either of them finding a life companion. The thought reminded him of his pressing problem.

"Can I speak to you both alone, in private?"

They looked at him with burning curiosity. "Of course," they said in unison.

Alexander led them out into Mrs. Penrose's garden before coming to an abrupt halt next to the cherry tree. As expected, his mind was instantly flooded with the memory of Eve. It seemed a fitting place to ask for their pledge.

"There is something I must ask of you," Alexander began. He could feel his heart beating hard in his chest.

"Don't tell me," Elliot said, showing his impatience. "You want us to accompany you to Bavaria. You want the golden-haired woman to turn Evelyn."

"No," Alexander cried, scowling to show his disgust and shaking his head to reaffirm his position. "I would never want that for Evelyn. If you had the plague, would you want to infect those you love?"

Elliot had the decency to look ashamed. "Bringing us out here … I just thought—"

"I want you to kill me," Alexander said quietly.

"Kill you!" both gentlemen said before their mouths fell open.

Elliot frowned. "But I thought you were happy with Evelyn?"

"I am so deliriously happy I can hardly contain it." Eve was his life. Nothing else mattered to him. "I want to make a pact. When Evelyn takes her last breath and is no longer of this world, I want you to kill me."

"But why?" Leo said. They were the words of someone who had never experienced great emotion. The depth of his feelings for Eve went beyond anything even he could comprehend, and he'd rather die than walk the nights alone.

Alexander smiled. "Because I do not want to live a day on this earth without her. Because I want to hold her in my arms for all eternity."

Elliot smirked. "Perhaps you should take up poetry as you have a very eloquent way with words."

"Does that mean you'll do it?"

"What if we make a pact, and you change your mind?" Leo asked.

"I won't. But if it eases your conscience, each year I will express my wishes in writing. Then there can be no mistaking my intention."

Elliot narrowed his gaze. "Does Evelyn know this is what you intend to do?"

"Not yet." He held out his hand to them. "I ask my brothers to take my hand and seal our pact."

Elliot looked at Leo. "I swore to honour the brotherhood, and so I must honour our brother's wishes."

"Very well." Leo nodded, and he shook Alexander's hand.

"You are an unusual man, Alexander," Elliot said, gripping his hand firmly. "But I swear to do as you ask." He paused and then added, "Besides, it means you'll always be part of the brotherhood. I had a sneaky suspicion you'd run away with your wife never to be heard from again."

Alexander smiled. "The thought had crossed my mind."

"Here you all are." Eve's voice cut through the darkness, and she came to stand next to him, threading her arm through his and hugging it tightly. "Forgive the intrusion but I've come to steal my husband away." She glanced at the cherry tree, a coy smile touching her lips and he knew what she was thinking.

Flicking his gaze towards the house, he silently dismissed

his friends. "We'll be in town for another week before we head back to Hampshire. I'll call on you before we leave."

"Come, Leo," Elliot said, draping his arm over his friend's shoulder. "Let's go inside and discuss our wager."

Once they were alone, Alexander drew Eve into an embrace and kissed her softly. "So, you've come to steal me away," he whispered against her mouth. "I can't wait to discover where we're going."

She looked up into his eyes, and he felt her love warm his soul. "It's somewhere you've been before," she said, taking his hand and pulling him down beneath the cherry tree, "a heavenly plane where our hearts can soar freely."

Bunching up her dress, she sat astride him.

"I always like it when you're in charge of the journey."

She gave a pleasurable hum as he rained kisses down her neck. "I hope all our nights will be as magical as this."

Alexander let the warmth of her love embrace him, his heart bursting with unimaginable joy. "Oh, I can promise you they will be."

Thank you for reading *Lost to the Night*

If you enjoyed this story and would like to read an excerpt
from the next book in the series
Slave to the Night
please turn the page.

You can find out more about the author at
adeleclee.com

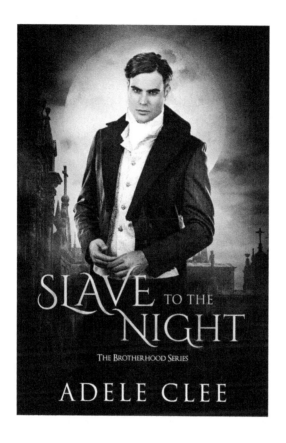

Viscount Markham has one rule — never bed the same woman twice.

But all rules are made to be broken.

CHAPTER 1

With trembling fingers, Grace Denton handed the invitation to the sour-faced majordomo and tried to offer a confident smile. He raised his bushy brows before studying the neat script. Thank the Lord she had the luxury of wearing a mask. It afforded anonymity while certain parts of her anatomy were blatantly exposed for all to see. Never in her life had she imagined baring so much flesh. Her breasts were almost bursting out of her sister's scandalous gown.

Under the servant's hawk-like gaze, she felt her control waver as doubt pushed to the fore.

What was she thinking?

No one would believe she was Caroline. It took more than a striking similarity to assume someone's identity. Her sister oozed confidence in every situation. Whereas Grace blushed like a berry whenever she felt nervous. Caroline spoke with poise and eloquence. Whereas she often rambled and muttered to herself and was prone to saying the wrong thing entirely.

"Enjoy your evening, miss."

"I'm sure I will," she replied, despite fearing it was highly inappropriate to converse with the servants.

As she stepped into the ballroom, she gasped in awe at the vibrant spectacle. The crowd shone in their flamboyant costumes, and she struggled to absorb the dazzling array of colours. Etiquette be damned at a masquerade, she thought, as milkmaids danced with knights and bishops and an Oriental princess partnered a sea captain.

Pushing through the crowd, she breathed a sigh of relief. She'd climbed the first obstacle, and now her toes were wedged into the foothold, even if she was dangling precariously from a precipice and could easily flounder.

Once the wife of a gentleman, she knew how to conduct herself in formal situations. But her education had taken place at garden parties and provincial assemblies. She had no real experience when it came to mingling with the aristocracy.

Her older sister, Caroline, had been in London for a year —as a paid companion to an elderly matron, or so Grace had thought. Even Mrs. Whitman had been fooled. Else, despite Grace being a widow of three-and-twenty, she would never have left her in Caroline's care.

Grace caught her reflection in one of the long mirrors lining the wall. The candlelight rebounded off the glass and cast a golden glow over her surprisingly voluptuous figure, squashed into the medieval-inspired gown. From the neck down she appeared exactly like all the other ladies: elegant and sophisticated with an air of wicked sensuality.

From the neck up, things hadn't quite gone to plan.

She had singed a few tendrils with the curling iron. They were crispy, and the smoky aroma invaded her nostrils whenever she turned her head. What had started out as an elaborate coiffure, looked more like a poorly made bird's nest. The pearl hair comb had slipped down and was digging into the back of her ear.

Hesitant feet caused her to amble around the ballroom. More than a few people turned their heads to acknowledge her. The mole on her left cheek—in the same place as Caroline's—coupled with her fiery red hair, no doubt convinced them of her identity. Yet despite feigning an air of composure, inside she felt like a child in a room full of hungry wolves.

Grace knew the name of her quarry, but nothing more. One word from the dissipated lord would confirm what she needed to know. After spending a lifetime with Caroline, she recognised the language of a liar, although she had no skill when it came to the mannerisms of a murderer.

"Caroline. There you are. I've been looking everywhere for you."

The warm, feminine voice caught her off guard. Grace swung around with a gasp, her fingers fluttering to her throat and coming to rest on the topaz necklace—another of her sister's prized possessions.

"Why, am I late?" Grace knew her voice lacked confidence, knew the lady before her was a stranger.

"No," the lady replied, her curious gaze roaming over Grace's hair. "You're not late. But Barrington is looking for you, and he is not best pleased. I thought I ought to warn you."

Grace recalled no mention of a Barrington in her sister's diary. There had been a whole host of unseemly tales regarding other gentlemen; so she had to suppose this man lacked the skills necessary to capture Caroline's attention.

Guilt flared.

Reading the evidence of someone's innermost thoughts was a gross invasion of privacy. She'd spent a whole day holding the book in her hands before finally deciding to peel back the cover and peer inside.

"And what have I done to warrant Barrington's displeasure?" Now she sounded far too haughty.

Oh, this was never going to work.

A frown marred the lady's brow. "Don't be coy. You know full well you were to meet him at the theatre last night. But looking at the state of your hair, it's clear you're not well."

"I do feel a little out of sorts." Feigning illness would go some way to account for her character flaws. And it gave her a perfect opportunity to broach the subject of her quarry. "I would have stayed at home tonight, but I need to speak to Lord Markham."

The lady made an odd puffing sound. "Markham? Don't waste your time. You know his rule about never bedding the same woman twice." She stepped closer. "Was he so good you would risk facing rejection?"

What was she supposed to say to that?

"He … he was so good I'd ride backwards on a donkey and cry *tallyho* just for another chance."

The lady screwed up her nose and then giggled. "What's wrong with you tonight? You're normally so serious."

"My heart's all jittery thinking about Lord Markham. Where is he? Have you seen him this evening?"

"He's standing near the alcove. Markham's the only gentleman in the room not in costume, so you're unlikely to miss him." The lady placed her hand on Grace's arm. "What are you going to do about Barrington? He will not tolerate your blasé attitude. Without the protection of a gentleman, he can make things difficult for you."

Grace did not have to worry about Barrington and neither did Caroline, not anymore.

"I'll do what I always do," she said, attempting to sound vain. "I shall smile and flutter my lashes and all will be well."

In their youth, Caroline had used the trick a hundred times or more.

"Oh, you're incorrigible. Let me know how you fare with

Lord Markham, although I'm sure to hear tales of your humiliation. I may even rouse the courage to try myself."

As Grace walked away, she was overcome by a wave of sadness. Was this how Caroline spent her time? Comparing conquests and juggling suitors? There was something shallow, something degrading about succumbing to the voracious demands of men.

Where had it all gone wrong?

After reading the diary, she had a fair idea.

There was only one gentleman wearing evening clothes. He was conversing with a man dressed in the garb of a Turkish prince, whose crimson pantaloons were attracting much female attention.

Lord Markham, or so she assumed, had the bearing of a man who bowed to no one. Dressed all in black, he exuded raw masculinity. With his arrogant chin, sinful mouth and lethal gaze he embodied all the qualities she imagined of a scandalous rake. His decision to forgo a mask made him appear all the more masterful, all the more dangerous.

Grace swallowed down her nerves and tried to muster just an ounce of her sister's steely composure. It was the height of rudeness to interrupt a conversation and so she hovered at his side in the hope he would notice her.

The first thing he did notice were her breasts and his lustful gaze lingered there for longer than necessary. Grace could feel her cheeks flame under his scrutiny. Her instincts cried for her to flee, the feeling only tempered by her sheer desperation to discover what the gentleman knew.

His expression altered dramatically as his gaze drifted up to the topaz necklace, up to the mole on her cheek. Recognition dawned, and his countenance resumed the same tired, world-weary air.

"Ah, Miss Rosemond," he said, glancing down at her breasts once more. "I see you have found a way to enhance the paltry assets bestowed upon you. Some poor devil will have a fright when his hand curls around a pair of old stockings."

The gentleman's mouth was as foul as his reputation. Trust him to notice the only distinct difference. And why had he called her Rosemond? Had he mistaken her for someone else or had Caroline used a different name? More importantly, he showed not the slightest surprise at her presence.

"You presume to know me, my lord," she said, trying not to show her displeasure at his derogatory remark. He apparently felt within his rights to speak in such base terms, and she felt another pang of sadness for the sweet sister she once knew.

The Turkish prince sniggered, his turban wobbling back and forth, but became distracted when a lady stopped to admire the softness of his silk trousers.

Lord Markham raised an arrogant brow. "I know you a little too well, I fear."

Grace lifted her chin. "How so? I find such a critical assessment causes my memory to fail me." She was doing far better than she ever hoped and resisted the urge to clap her hands. After all, such a dire situation was not to be trivialised.

"When it comes to the weaknesses of the flesh, my memory never fails me."

Grace smiled. "I'm afraid I can only recall the things I deem important."

Lord Markham narrowed his gaze, and his mouth twitched at the corners. "Then tell me what you do remember."

The request caught her by surprise.

How was she supposed to answer that?

"I-I couldn't p-possibly repeat it."

Oh, God, she was going to start mumbling.

Lord Markham turned fully and focused his attention,

gazing deeply through the oval holes of her mask into her eyes. The room appeared to sway, and she sucked in a breath to calm the flutter in her heart.

"Oh, I think you can," he said. The amber flecks in his green eyes grew more prominent. His gloved finger came to rest on her pendant, drifted seductively over the topaz stones. Grace shivered at his touch and his mouth curved up into a satisfied smile. "Tell me what you imagine occurred between us. Tell me."

Grace swallowed. "I … I won't repeat it."

He leant forward. The smell of pine and some other earthy masculine fragrance bombarded her senses. "Tell me." He dropped his hand as his greedy gaze dipped to her breasts bulging out from the neckline of her gown. "Whisper the words to me."

Little streams of light blurred her vision, forcing her to blink rapidly. Her mind felt fuzzy as though a dense fog had settled to obscure all rational thought. All she could think of was how it felt to lie naked with a man.

But not just any man—with Lord Markham.

Good heavens.

Beads of perspiration formed on her brow, and she touched her fingers to her forehead as strange words unwittingly entered her thoughts.

But there was murder afoot. She was convinced of it. The thought gave her the strength to fight whatever weird and wonderful notion filled her head.

She was here for Caroline. Nothing else mattered.

"I-I don't remember anything," she whispered, her breath coming short and quick as she dismissed the image of her eager fingers roaming over his muscular chest.

The muscle in his cheek twitched. He jerked his head back with a look of utter bewilderment. Had no one ever refused his request? Knowing she had the power to knock the arrogance out of him, gave her the courage to be bold.

"Nor will I waste my time or imagination pandering to your warped sense of curiosity. If you're looking for someone to indulge your fantasies, I suggest you try …" Her mind went blank. Where do gentlemen find women to frolic with, other than at a ball? "Try the … the market."

It was the first thing that popped into her head. You could buy everything at the market, why not women?

Lord Markham's eyes widened. "The market?"

While her blood rushed through her veins at a rapid rate, it decided to take a detour past her cheeks, choosing her ears to convey her embarrassment. She could feel them swelling, throbbing and burning. If she were to touch them with wet fingers, they would most certainly sizzle.

"I am a viscount," he continued with an indolent wave. "I do not need to trawl the markets looking for someone to warm my bed, as well you know."

"Forgive me," she said, overcome with a desperate need to wipe the smirk off his face. "What else was I supposed to think when you have the mouth of a sewer rat?"

"This is an interesting game," he said, showing no sign of offence. "I cannot recall the last time my mind was as stimu-lated as my—"

"I do not need to hear more of your vulgarity."

He put his hand on his chest and laughed. "My vulgarity? Have you cared to glance in the mirror? Your hair gives the impression that you've recently been tumbled. Your gown is far too small and at any moment. I am in danger of being blinded. Your lips are red and swollen from—"

"It is rouge," she said, thrusting her hands on her hips. At least, she hoped that's what was in the silver cachou box. Their mother had often said such things were nought but selfish vanity to mask a weak mind. "And I have put on weight since I last wore this dress. There is nothing vulgar or lewd about any of it."

"Are you not a courtesan, Caroline? Do you not openly court vulgarity?"

Grace suppressed a gasp upon hearing her sister's name pass from his lips. She knew the depths of Caroline's disgrace but saying it so openly made it seem so crude, so terribly heartbreaking.

"I am a lady, my lord," she said, unable to control the anger that infused her tone, "and I ask you to have a care. I have tolerated your uncouth manner for long enough."

When he smiled, she knew she had made a mistake.

Lord Markham bowed. "Please accept my humble apology." There was not even a hint of sarcasm in his tone. A shiver raced down her spine as she suspected her worst fear was about to come to fruition. "I'm afraid your deception forced me to be blunt."

"My … my deception? Now you're speaking in riddles, my lord."

"Despite wearing her necklace, I think we both know you're not Caroline Rosemond. The question is who the hell are you, and what do you want with me?"

Printed in Great Britain
by Amazon